Missing in Bangkok

J.G. Barrie

Cover Design: Dan Huckle

Dedication

To Jonah and Maxine. More lights in my universe.
.

Table of Contents

Chapter 1...1
Chapter 2...9
Chapter 3..14
Chapter 4..16
Chapter 5..23
Chapter 6..26
Chapter 7..29
Chapter 8..34
Chapter 9..39
Chapter 10...45
Chapter 11...53
Chapter 12...57
Chapter 13...62
Chapter 14...70
Chapter 15...74
Chapter 16...81
Chapter 17...88
Chapter 18...93
Chapter 19...97
Chapter 20..101
Chapter 21..104
Chapter 22..107
Chapter 23..111
Chapter 24..118
Chapter 25..123
Chapter 26..129
Chapter 27..137
Chapter 28..141
Chapter 29..144
Chapter 30..151
Chapter 31..156
Chapter 32..163
Chapter 33..167

Chapter 34 174
Chapter 35 178
Chapter 36 185
Chapter 37 191
Chapter 38 195
Chapter 39 198
Chapter 40 202
Chapter 41 209
Chapter 42 216
Chapter 43 221
Chapter 44 226
Chapter 45 233
Chapter 46 241
Chapter 47 251
Chapter 48 258
Chapter 49 262
Chapter 50 265
Chapter 51 280
About the Author..285
Other books by J.G. Barrie...287

Chapter 1

Fall in Calgary. A carpet of yellow, orange and red rolled gently up the foothills to the Rocky Mountains to the west of the city. The peaks cut a jagged edge against the bright blue sky. It was a good day to die. He didn't know that yet.

Taking in the scene from the twenty-first floor of an office building in downtown Calgary, Ben Guthrie could not help but feel blessed. Blessed by his luck with founding a successful small company in Calgary and blessed by his happy marriage.

His gaze shifted from the distant mountains in a haze of blue, to the eyes of the slightly tanned woman in a photograph on his desk. Smiling out at him was his beloved wife, Jessica, who had just celebrated her milestone fortieth birthday. Her impish smile still made his heart race, even after twenty years of marriage. They had met at the Mariposa Festival in Ontario. She, with her white cotton dress and a ring of flowers that crowned her tousled dark hair and he with his tattered blue jeans. They had been among young people who danced and swayed to the music of a fading hippie generation.

She had introduced him to her parents two weeks after they had met. She was their only child. Jessica resembled her mother of Anglo-Indian origin, who had migrated to Canada shortly after the Partition of India and Pakistan. She was tall, elegant and slim with a dimpled cheek, but hair now grey. Within two years Ben and Jessica had married. It was a small wedding. Karen, her room-mate and best friend, had been her bridesmaid.

Ben loved their home in Crescent Heights which overlooked downtown Calgary. It still resonated with the music of Leonard Cohen, Joan Baez and John Lennon. Jessica's experience as a landscape designer had transformed their home to look like a show home. He remembered that he had carried the rocks for the rock garden in the front yard, dug the hole, and poured concrete for the small pond. Jessica had planted pussy willows and lilac bushes along the back fence. In the summer, the garden blossomed with petunias, rose bushes and nasturtiums. Blue spruce trees towered over a mountain ash underneath which their garden swing nestled. The garden swing, where eighteen years ago he had rocked with Carol, their daughter, cradled in his arms. He was so proud of Carol. Free spirited, optimistic and a joy to be with. She would enter university this year after having spent a year volunteering at an orphanage in India.

Life had been good to Ben.

The door opened and Len Green walked in.

"Ben! Guess what? We were the lowest bid."

"The bid for the Bow River pedestrian bridge? Yes!" Ben leaped out of his chair. Smiling broadly, he shook Len's hand vigorously.

"Len! This is a huge contract! The largest we won this year! Finally! And right here in Calgary!"

Len felt Ben loosen his grip on his hand. His broad smile suddenly changed to a grimace. He looked like he was in pain. His face turned pale and then blue. Len grabbed him before he fell to the floor. Beads of sweat erupted from Ben's face.

"Ben!"

"Can't breathe... call...help." Ben grew limp in his arms.

He grabbed Ben's phone and called 911. He lifted him off the floor so that he could lie more comfortably on the couch, loosened his belt and tie and shouted, "Pam! Come quick!"

Pam looked at Ben, turned pale and held her hand against her mouth. Temporary paralysis had set in as she watched her boss obviously in intense pain.

"Go to the front! I've already called 911. They should be here any minute!" Len barked.

"Len..."

"Ben, take it easy. Help is on the way."

Ben clutched his chest again. The pain was more intense. He was fading. He could hear Len's voice but it was as if it was from far away. Farther and farther.

The pain subsided but he felt weak. The pain had gone. He felt alone. At peace. He heard music and bells. He was in Winnipeg. Visiting Jessica and her parents for Christmas dinner. Then they were singing carols by the tree. He could only hear Jessica's voice. Soft, soothing and melodious.

Then it was Jessica again, holding a newborn baby girl on a hospital bed, tears of joy streaming down her face while he hugged her and gently kissed his little infant. She was saying something but it was muffled. He could not see her face. Suddenly Jessica appeared.

He must have fallen asleep. Jessica was speaking to him in her gentle voice. Rubbing his forehead and kissing his cheek. He tasted her salty tears.

"What happened? Where am I?" he asked with a start, looking at Jessica and the unfamiliar surroundings.

"In the Foothills Hospital, my love. You'll be okay. Len came by to the home and brought me here."

"What happened?"

"They think you had a heart attack. It was lucky Len came into your office at that moment."

Ben opened his mouth to say something but no words came out.

"Don't worry, my love. Rest. Sleep if you want. I am with you. As I've always been."

Once again Ben heard the music. The soft tinkle of bells. A harp. A child giggling. The sounds were barely audible to him.

"Help!" screamed Jessica as she rushed out of the room.

"He turned blue. He's not breathing!" She yelled again for the persons at the nursing station.

A nurse pressed the alarm bell and the doctor came in a few moments. He placed an oxygen mask on Ben's mouth. He struck his chest a few times and then turned to Jessica.

"Please leave us with him for a few moments, Mrs. Guthrie. We'll try to revive him."

They closed the curtains around his bed. Jessica waited in the hallway as Carol came running towards her.

"Mum! What happened? Is Dad okay? Pam called to tell me to come here." Jessica hugged her and didn't let go. Carol felt her mother's body tremble. She was fearful of losing her father. Carol said nothing. Then, as she wiped the tears from her eyes and cheek, Jessica saw the doctor and nurse come out of the room.

"I'm sorry, Mrs. Guthrie. He had another heart attack. It sometimes follows after the first one. We couldn't revive him." He gently touched

5

her shoulder and led her back to the hospital bed. Carol followed.

Ben lay there, pale and lifeless. Jessica sobbed as she held his still warm face in her hands, kissed him on the lips, stroked his cheeks which were wet with her tears. Carol held his hand with both of hers and cried softly on his chest. The nurse and the doctor stood silently watching the wife and daughter of this man whom they couldn't help. They left them so that the family, what was left of it, could be alone together.

Len was waiting to hear about Ben's condition while he was seated in the lobby of the hospital.

"Are you a relative?" asked the Admissions Receptionist.

"No, he's my boss."

"Sorry, sir. Only family members can visit him."

"I brought his wife here. She is with him now. I'll wait outside."

A breeze carried falling leaves past his feet as he struggled to control his emotions. *This can't be happening. He's too young. What would the company be without Ben? Why him and not me? I drink, smoke and am overweight. It's not fair."*

He sat down on a bench outside the hospital entrance. He expelled his breath in a long sigh and dropped his shoulders. An older lady sitting on the next bench smiled at him.

"Don't worry," she said, "this is a good hospital. They will take good care of your wife."

"I'm not married," Len said.

"Oh? Is it a sibling then?"

"No, my boss."

"You must really like him."

"He's the best. I've been with him for the last twenty-five years. From when he started the company. My boss is the owner, salesman and manager. We were a small outfit and now we have a hundred employees. Happy employees. All because of that good man in Emergency right now."

"Was it an accident? Or is he an older man?"

"No, he's in his forties. It seems to have been a heart attack. This shouldn't have happened to him. He is in excellent shape. Not like me."

Len drew a tissue from his pocket and wiped his cheeks.

"Oh, so sorry. He is so young. Don't worry he will fight back."

Len looked at his scuffed shoes. "Yes, he is a fighter. He is like an older brother to me. I must leave now."

He nodded to the woman and walked to his grey Buick. He sat behind the wheel, sighed and turned on the ignition. The car rattled as he left the parking lot. He had to have that loose muffler attended to. The muffler was the least of his problems. He would soon find out that Ben had just died.

Chapter 2

Jessica and Carol were picking at the food on their plate, munching silently. Snowflakes pelted the window as the wind whistled through the stand of spruce trees in the back yard.

"It's been almost a year now, Mum. I still miss him so much."

"Yes, Honey. It still seems like it was only last week that we were at the Foothills. So much has changed."

Guthrie Construction had been sold after Ben died. Jessica did not regret selling it; she could not run the company and had no desire to do so. Nobody could do the job better than Ben. Besides she could never have returned to that office and stayed for any length of time.

"Mum?"

Jessica snapped back to the present.

"Sorry, Honey..."

"You really are drinking too much these days. You didn't drink when Dad was alive."

Jessica swirled the ice cubes in her glass. "Your father should never have introduced me to Scotch."

"Muu--um! You know what I mean. That's half the bottle this evening!"

"Please don't give me advice, Carol! I can hold my liquor!" Jessica took another swallow from her glass without looking at Carol. Her daughter was right. She had been drinking too much. Loneliness was doing it to her.

Carol sipped her ginger ale, bubbles collapsing in her mouth. "I need a change, Mum."

"Why? Because of me?"

"No, Mum. I want to travel."

"California?"

"No, farther away. I was looking for a summer job and found that they needed English teachers in Bangkok. Thought it would be cool, teaching foreign kids how to speak English. That was one of the things I did at a work-term in Bangalore when I helped at that orphanage."

"Bangkok? Why on earth would you want to go there?"

"I'd like to see what Thailand is like. I hear that the people are really nice." She ate silently, looking at her mother as she poured another drink into her glass. "Besides I want to be away for a while. It may help my missing Dad..."

How could she do this to me? I need her. She needs me too...

"Mum? You don't seem too keen about this. You weren't concerned when I went to India."

"Carol...Honey... is it hard to live with me? Is it the drinking? I can stop tomorrow. Promise..." she got up and spilled her drink. "Shit! Look what you made me do!"

"Mu-um..." Carol didn't want to talk about her mother's newly acquired drinking problem again.

"I had hoped you would go to University here. If not in Calgary, maybe in Vancouver." She said as she soaked up the spill with a paper towel. "Your dad left you a lot of money. For your education, a new car, an apartment if you want it. You can do so much with that money. You don't need to travel to Thailand! Besides it is so dangerous there!"

I shouldn't be so negative...my little girl needs to grow up. She needs to be away from me. I wish she would stay closer though. I should join AA.

"Mum. I don't need so much money. There are many people in Thailand who have nothing. Mum, you really need to travel to some of these places. The people there don't have what we have here."

"You want to give your money to people in Thailand?" Jessica was surprised that came out the way it did but was glad she didn't blurt: *what about the poor people in Calgary, or Canada? Don't they need you here too?*

"No. I just want to go there. It will be so different. I want to teach young children. I like it. Maybe study Education in University when I return. You can come later and spend a few months with me, Mum. Get to know some poor people."

Jessica picked up her fork again and nibbled at her food, trying to appear relaxed. She rose from the table and poured the remainder of her drink down the sink.

Now I'm supposed to feel guilty about having so much money. She probably wants me to make a large donation to the school in Thailand that's what. Jessica! Be more positive!

"It's OK, Honey. I wish I had done that when I was young. Never left North America! Thought everything I ever needed was here. Skiing in the mountains, the California and Florida experience. Our condo in Hawaii in winter. And I never even visited my mum's home in Agra, even though I am an Anglo-Indian and should have experienced some of my heritage first-hand."

"You're OK with it then? We can email each other often. Maybe you can have Karen stay with you for a while when I am gone."

"Yes, Honey. Go ahead and make your plans. Maybe I will visit you when you settle in."

Carol held her mother's hands and kissed her cheek.

"Mum, I'm so sorry. I miss Dad so much. He wanted me to travel. He was right, I will learn so much about people. You understand, don't you?"

Understand she did. Carol had given her companionship when she needed it after losing Ben. She was all she had for family.

In the weeks that followed, Carol made her plans, clearly excited by her upcoming adventure in a place that was going to be so different. The day of her departure came quickly, perhaps too quickly.

Chapter 3

Eighteen months later, Jessica read Carol's latest email that detailed the exploits of the children whom she taught in Bangkok. When she began her reply, the doorbell rang. She was surprised to find a slightly-built, young Asian woman, standing on her doorstep.

"Mrs. Guthrie? Mrs. Jessica Guthrie?" She seemed to struggle with the language.

"Yes?"

"So sorry show up like this," the woman said. "I wanted to phone but not found your number."

"How can I help you?"

"My name Jariya Panya. I come from Bangkok. Carol in trouble."

Oh God, why else would a Thai girl show up on my doorstep? Is Carol pregnant and she didn't tell me?

She invited her in.

"I glad we meet," Jariya said. "When I get call, I think I write you. Then I get travel visa and come see you instead. It is not good with Carol."

"I'm glad you came," Jessica said. She wondered what Jariya was talking about and why Carol hadn't mentioned anything about her problems in her emails.

"I want thank you and family. What Carol did for me, so very, very kind." She began to tear up and found a tissue in her purse. "Her gift so very kind for me."

"Well, that's very nice, Jariya," Jessica said. "What exactly was it that Carol gave you? What was this gift?"

"She gave me money every month, but I not see her for many days. I think something bad happened to her," she said. "Before she gone, I saw two men outside restaurant where I work. I saw them follow Carol one day. They seemed bad people."

Jessica stared at her.

"I'm sorry, Jariya. I don't understand. Are you sure it is my Carol who is missing?"

"Yes. She come my restaurant every day after school. Had meal there and then went home. She not come anymore. She must have been taken by those men." Jariya removed a photograph from her purse. "I show you. This picture of Carol she gave me. This your Carol, yes?"

Jessica could barely breathe as Jariya handed over the photograph. She stared at it and felt the air sucked from the room.

Oh, God, she thought. *This can't be true.*

Chapter 4

The photograph was indeed that of Carol, her beloved daughter. She was among a group of young children who were her students. Through tear filled eyes, still in shock, she looked again at the picture, hoping it may be someone who looked liked Carol instead. The eyes were those of her daughter and so was that beautiful smile. But how could this be?

Jessica held her head in her hands and closed her eyes. Was this a bad dream? Is this really happening? It can't be. If Carol had been kidnapped, how could she be sending emails? Would the authorities not inform the Canadian embassy that one of their citizens was missing? How could she not be informed? Carol had all her papers with her to indicate her permanent home address. Why was she not advised?

She looked at Jariya. *Could this be a joke or a hoax?*

"I must be alone for awhile. Can you come back tomorrow?" asked Jessica.

"Sure, sure. I come tomorrow. I not far away."

Jariya held Jessica's hands as she escorted her to the door. Jariya hugged her and closed the door behind her.

She immediately went back to the computer and read the last email from Carol.

Hi Mum, its hard to believe that I have been here going on two years. It seems like only last week that I arrived. The monsoons will be starting soon and I recall it was quite an experience last year. What we have in Calgary is merely a drizzle compared to this. I wish you were here. I have so many sights to show you. The email system in Bangkok is slow and not very reliable. My message drafts get lost when the power goes off, which happens now and then. That's why I keep my emails brief. More next week.

Love,

Carol

She read the previous week's email:

Hi Mum,

Last week I went with some friends to Phuket. We took the bus, which was cheaper than renting a car. Although Emily and Millie can drive, they prefer not to, since the drivers are too aggressive and the streets are too crowded. They also drive on the wrong side of the road here.

It was beautiful at the beach. The water was sooo warm and it was sooo relaxing. Can you visit me soon? I want to stay here for another year."
Love,
Carol

Jessica scrolled through other emails. All of them were short, all of them happy. There really must be a mistake. But it was definitely Carol's picture. How did Jariya get it? Come to think of it, how could she afford a trip from Thailand to Calgary? She did not seem rich, she looked like one of those migrants who worked the fields in British Columbia.

Jessica walked to the window. She did not recall hearing, or seeing, a car which may have brought Jariya here. All she had heard was the doorbell ring. With her keen sense of smell, she did not detect a perfume, or any other body odour of any recent visitor to her home. Normally she could smell perfumes or odours long after people had left. She now started to panic. Did that really happen? Have I been drinking too much?

She opened the door to look out on the path to see if there was any sign of her visitor, but there was none. She walked down the path to the street hoping that she may still be around. Since there was no sign of her, she went back into her house to get her car keys. She drove around the block and down Crescent Heights Drive but could not see any sign of Jariya. *Why didn't I ask her where she was staying?! How stupid of me!* But then, with the shock of her daughter's possible kidnapping she excused her mistake.

The nearest motel was five kilometres down Centre Street. She pulled into the Happy Traveller Inn, walked to the reception and was greeted by a cheery young lady.

"Good morning, madam. Would you like a room? Do you need someone to help with your luggage in your car?"

"No thank you. I need to talk to one of your guests."

"And the name is?"

"I believe the last name is Panya. A young girl, Jariya. Jariya Panya. She had an accent but I believe that was how she pronounced it. Jar-Rear Pan-Yah."

"Let me check. No, we don't have a Panya registered. Are you sure of the name? Do you know how it is spelled?"

"I'm not sure. She just arrived from Bangkok, Thailand."

"No, all our registered guests have given us American or Canadian home addresses. We have not had any Asian guests this week."

"Alright, thank you. I must be in the wrong place."

"You can use the phone in the lobby to call the other hotels if you wish madam."

"Thank you. I need to go home first."

Perhaps she came straight from the airport. But no, Jariya did mention that she was not far from here. This was the only motel that was not far from her home. Where else could she be staying?

Back at home, she wrote a short email to Carol. *Hi Honey. Please email me asap. Have some news for you. Love, Mum.*

It was hard to concentrate. She still did not believe what had just happened. *Had she dozed off and dreamt that?* She sniffed the remains of her coffee mug. It was just coffee, not Scotch. She never drank in the morning. Her Scotch was for the evening only. One, maybe two shots, sometimes three. She had cut back after Carol had left for Thailand.

She was getting suspicious. Maybe this was a hoax after all. But why? Why would someone pull such a cruel joke? She should have talked more to Jariya and not sent here away so soon. She could not communicate with persons of other cultures despite her own heritage. Her mother had never spoken of any relatives in India and did not follow any customs that may have been part of her upbringing. Jessica felt that she, herself, had always been too patronizing or too superficial when talking to persons of other races. Not that she disliked them or anything. Just not used to talking to them. All her friends, and Ben's friends, were at least third generation Canadians, Americans or

British. The private school she went to in Winnipeg was limited to the very rich and did not have any immigrants. She had limited knowledge of other cultures and her only exposure to another culture had been during her occasional trips to Mexico. All their family vacations had been in the US or Canada. They had never even been to Europe!

She went back to the computer and Googled 'Thailand'. Fortunately, her few computer skills included Google Searches. The King's Cup Elephant Polo tournament was on. A Music Festival and a Mekong River Boat Festival. *What language do they speak? Is Thai a language or do they speak a version of Chinese?* She was frustrated by her lack of knowledge of countries outside North America. She checked her email to see if Carol had replied but there was no response. She spent most of the day at the computer, researching Thailand and checking if Carol had responded. Soon it was the late afternoon but she had made no progress.

Jessica wanted to visit Karen, her close friend on the other side of town. But what would she tell her? *Did Jariya Panya even visit me this morning? There will surely be a message from Carol in the morning.*

The simple meal of canned tuna and a salad was untouched. Rick Mercer's rant on CBC failed to interest her and she surfed channels but could not concentrate. Lying down on the bed was useless as she was wound up like a clock spring, *a cuckoo clock spring* she thought. Memories of her last farewell to Carol at the airport, her last birthday party, times she fell sick, all filled her mind as she tossed and turned in her bed.

She got up and turned the TV set on again. Images and voices, voices and images, all with no meaning. Empty laughter on the sitcoms. She checked her email again. Nothing. Fear and anguish tormented her. She wished she had someone to talk to. *Ben! I need you!*

Out of her window she gazed at the sky which had slowly changed to pink. Robins were singing. She had not slept a wink. Still wound up. No messages from Carol on her email. Only the usual Junk Mail. She had a breakfast of toast and jam with her coffee, got dressed and waited for her visitor in the living room, watching the street outside her window. Maybe the girl would return.

There was a thump on the door and she jumped up. It was only the newspaper. Nine o'clock, ten o'clock, eleven. Every car coming down the street would make Jessica rush to the window but the cars just drove by. She now doubted that Jariya Panya had even visited. She checked her email. Nothing from Carol.

She did not hear the doorbell ring, nor the timid knocks on the door. Neither did she hear the mailbox open and close. Later she would read the handwritten letter which would suck her soul out of her body.

Chapter 5

Jessica opened the door and breathed in the fresh air deeply, happy that the nightmare was just that. She waved to her neighbour Janice who was walking her dog. It was a good day to be alive. She knew that it must have been her imagination. Probably drank more than usual the night before that imaginary visit. Jessica opened her mailbox to check for the usual bills and junk mail. Among these, an envelope with her name, handwritten, caught her eye and her heart thumped against her ribs. There was no address, only her name 'Missus Guthrie'. Her fingers trembled as she took the mail into the house, sat on the sofa, and separated the unusual envelope from the rest of the mail. She closed her eyes as a strong sense of foreboding overcame her. She opened her eyes, looked up and said softly *"Dear God, please help me."*

With shaking hands, she opened the envelope, and read the note, written on a sheet of lined paper, probably taken from a student's exercise book.

Dear Missus Guthrie,

I very sorry made you sad. You must come Bangkok soon. Carol is in danger. I came see you but no answer. I now must go back to Thailand. Please visit me there. Address: 2234 Thoet Thai 20, Bangkok.

Your friend and Carol's,

Jariya

She re-read the note. It was true. She <u>did</u> have a visitor yesterday. It was not her mind playing tricks on her. What was she to do? Carol was her only child. She must find her.

Jessica went back to the computer to check for an email from Carol. Nothing. She stared at the Inbox helplessly. She refreshed the screen a few times and still there was nothing new. She must go to Bangkok. She needed a companion. Should she ask Karen? Would Karen be a help, or a liability in a strange country? She probably should travel with a man. This would make more sense in a foreign country in the Far East. She had no male relatives who could travel with her. Alternatively, she could ask Karen to perhaps suggest alternatives for a travel partner. It was too early to phone her, so she shot off an email to Karen.

'Hi Karen, can I visit you today? I have something urgent to discuss.'

She remembered that Karen was not the type of person who checked her emails often. This was a problem. Her phone line had still not been repaired. After checking the computer a few times, she decided to go shopping to pick up some chocolates and flowers in case Karen responded that she could visit. Jessica rinsed her face, looked in the mirror at her puffy eyes tinged with red. Anyone could see she had been crying. She grabbed her purse and car keys, put on her sunglasses and opened the garage door and started her car. She needed a change of scene. Even a grocery store would do.

Chapter 6

Len Green pecked away at the keyboard but his mind was elsewhere. He needed a change. This was a shitty job. The Insurance Industry did not appeal to him but it was the only position available to him when Guthrie Construction was sold after Ben's death. Guthrie was not the same after Ben died. Len remembered the nastiness of the new Chief Engineer who had been appointed by the new owners.

"Len! Can you come to my office? Right away!" The guy was the cousin of the owner. He had insufficient experience in the business but loved to wield the power of his position.

His neck hair still bristled when he recalled that tone. *Go fuck yourself* is what he felt like telling the asshole. Instead, he tolerated it for a month. He left on his own citing that he had a better opportunity in another line of business. He didn't want to burn his bridges in the engineering industry. It was a small community. Lots of potential backstabbing could be done in the local clubs in Calgary frequented by these upstart young professionals.

It was almost five p.m. and this was the time that he and others in the office left for home. Quite unlike Guthrie Construction where most of the employees were not clock watchers. Even though Len was not really a 'people person' he enjoyed being in the company of gregarious and outgoing people.

Packing his briefcase with some files to review at home, he left the office and drove to pick up some food at the grocery store. He was checking the 'best before' dates on the tags on the bread bags when someone touched his shoulder lightly. It was Jessica Guthrie! He had last seen her at Ben's funeral.

"Len?"

"Oh! Hello, Jessica!"

"Still a bachelor, I guess? Doing your weekly, or is it daily, groceries?"

"I still like to create. But my dinner creations are not like my engineering designs unfortunately." Humorous comebacks were difficult for Len but he was glad to have managed one.

"Len, I have a bit of a problem and maybe you can help. You did great things for Ben and maybe you're the right guy to give me advice on a problem I am having."

Len was suspicious. He could not believe why Jessica would suddenly require his help when she had never contacted him after the company was sold.

"Are you hungry?" she asked.

"Yes, I forgot to defrost my hamburger at home and I do need a quick meal. Maybe it will be a cheese sandwich tonight for me."

"Cheese sandwich? Oh, Len, that sounds so bland. There's a nice place to eat two blocks from here. Would you like to join me for dinner? I don't like eating alone in a restaurant."

Len hesitated.

"Oh Len, please. You don't have to help but can you listen to what I have to say first?"

Len started to panic but it appeared he had little choice. He did not want to appear rude. "Oh sure, I guess I can pass on the cheese sandwich tonight. Had one for lunch today."

"Good. We can finish our shopping and meet in the parking lot. You can follow me to the restaurant. It's called Oscars."

Len had not expected to meet Jessica so soon, but he knew that sooner or later, the meeting was inevitable. He was not sure how much she knew about him and how much he resented her for selling the company.

This could be a nasty dinner date.

Chapter 7

"This way please." The hostess led them to a table by the window. "Your waiter today will be Ron. He'll be with you in a moment."

Jessica smiled and nodded. Len looked out the window to momentarily avoid eye contact with Jessica. He was as nervous as she was.

How did this damn woman corner me? he thought. He was stupid in not coming up with an excuse to pass on the dinner.

"Nice of you to join me, Len." She fidgeted with the cutlery on the table.

Len's blue plaid jacket did not match his flowered shirt or his green slacks. It appeared that there was no woman in his life to provide him with some suggestions for matching clothing. But then again, he was an engineer, who cared little about coordinated clothes. She had noticed that with some other technical people at Guthrie Construction. Jessica did not believe Len had ever been married.

"Something to drink?" Ron, the waiter, politely interrupted.

"A glass of red wine, please."

"You will love our house wine today. It is an Australian Shiraz."

"Yes, please, I'll have a glass. Wine for you too, Len?"

"Just a glass of water, thank you."

Len's cellphone rang much to his relief. He mumbled to be excused and left to go outside.

Jessica's nervousness abated after she took a sip of the wine that the waiter had placed on the table. It was good. Maybe she should drink Shiraz instead of Scotch at home. Moderately of course.

Len returned and appeared more relaxed.

"Sorry, that was a call from someone from the office. They want me to work this weekend." He sat down, took a sip of water and opened the menu. He could not concentrate on the menu items and waited for Jessica to comment. *This was a bad idea.* All he needed was a hamburger and fries and the menu appeared too sophisticated to include fast food items.

"Quite a selection," she said, having already made up her mind to have a rib steak and baked potato. *How can I ask him to travel with me? He may get the wrong impression.*

Fortunately, the waiter was there and made some suggestions regarding some of the Specials and his personal favourites. They each placed their order and the waiter nodded and left them alone for the next gambit.

Len hoped that Jessica did not notice his fingers trembling slightly as he held the menu. He still could not imagine how she had chanced to meet him and how much she knew about his resentment of her selling Guthrie Engineering.

"Miss the old job?"

"Very much! I've never had a better job. Besides, Ben was the best! We enjoyed working together and seeing our designs on paper being transformed to real structures and real buildings." Len visualized the bright steel and heavy cables and the rhythmic thud of the pile driver. He could almost feel the rumble of large earth-moving equipment. The sound of heavy equipment was his music, his life and his call. People were regretfully, a necessity to get his work done. People other than Ben, of course. And here he was with Jessica of all people. *Was she thinking of buying back the company and have him run it for her? The timing was off but perhaps he could do it after two years away from his favourite work.*

"Len, do you remember Carol?" Len's mind came back to this unpleasant meeting.

"Carol. Your daughter, of course. Ben often spoke of her."

"Well, she's in trouble."

"Oh? Boy friend issues?"

"No, something far more serious."

"Is she pregnant?"

Jessica fidgeted, her nails dug into her palms and she exhaled slowly. Len sipped his glass of water as she related the event of the previous day.

"Have you called the police?"

"No. The police here can do nothing and I don't know what the police are like in Bangkok." She paused to hear if he would ask how he could help.

Len fidgeted with the napkin. Ron returned and placed the entrees on the table.

"Bacon and chives for your potato?" he added some garnishing and then went away.

This woman comes to me of all people to ask for help. What should I do?

Len was beginning to regret this chance meeting. But he had to offer some help. Jessica was, after all, Ben's wife. "Well, there is something I can do for you. I have a former business contact in Bangkok who I can ask to help you. He works for a Security outfit in Bangkok."

Jessica put down her fork and hoped that Len didn't notice her quiet sigh of relief. "A Security Outfit? Great! Len, he may have some good contacts with the police. When can you get in touch with him? I'll pay any phone costs."

"That won't be necessary. I will call and ask him to dig into this, but you need to give me a recent photo of Carol, her birth date, where she is staying and any other details. I am sure he will find her and tell me that all is well. The woman who visited you was likely part of a local criminal network with contacts in Bangkok."

Jessica promised Len that she would bring the photo and other details to his office in the morning. After finishing the meal, she drove home, pleased with herself.

There was something stuck in her mailbox. Looked like a bird. Black tail feathers stuck out from under the lid. She opened the box. An icicle pierced her heart. A dead crow had been shoved in the box with its beak stuck through a folded piece of paper.

Chapter 8

They were there again. Their usual spot by the banyan tree outside the school. They were the human snakes not different from the roots of the tree than crept down to the path. Menacing and evil.

"Hello half-breed."

"Find your father yet?"

"Maybe you have many other brothers and sisters in Bangkok you don't know about. Your mother fucked all the tourists." They laughed and shoved him out of the way.

Always the derisive laughter. The same two boys, in one of the higher classes, trying to pick a fight with him. Anurak had to tolerate this on his way home from school every few days. One day, if there was only one of them, he would take him on. But he couldn't fight two at the same time. They were much bigger than he was.

His lighter skin and light eyes may have come from his father. 'Dad' was likely a *farang*, perhaps an American. During the Viet Nam war the U.S. was allowed to use bases in Thailand to support the war effort. Similar children roamed the streets of Bangkok looking for favours. He would not be surprised if one day, his mother, Taneka, were to tell him more. He never met his father and Taneka never spoke of him. One day he would ask her.

Slurs about being a half-breed or a bastard had hurt him deeply when he was younger. Not anymore. His fair skin had thickened with the constant insults.

The month of May was humid and hot in the city. Diesel fumes from buses and trucks frequently fogged the area. Acrid fumes and the smell of urine coming from the over-crowded streets did not make this a pleasant part of the city to live in. None of this bothered Anurak. He had grown up here and this was home. He entertained himself by watching tourists meander down this busy street, dressed in their colourful clothes which they had purchased during the first few days of their visit.

At age twelve he occasionally operated a souvenir shop owned by his mother. The little shop was outside the main business area. Bargain-hunting tourists ventured away from the security of downtown Bangkok with its gleaming skyscrapers and manicured parks to pick up local souvenirs outside the city core where they believed they could get lower prices. *Funny how the rich people always look for bargains. They spend lots of money to get here and then quibble about a few baht.*

'Anu' his mother would say 'one day you will run this shop by yourself. In school you will learn how to run a good business and you will make more money than your mother did.'

He enjoyed the school because he was in love. Miss Carol was a Canadian teacher. He looked forward to each school day so that he could gaze at her beautiful form and fantasize about them being alone in the class one day. He imagined she would take him on her lap and cuddle him and whisper endearments into his ear. But she had not been at the school for the last few days. Each morning he would wait at his desk hoping she would walk in. Instead, it was a substitute.

The last time he saw her was when she was talking to a man who appeared to be having some trouble. Perhaps he was the father of one of the students, explaining why his son was not at school that day. They had walked into the street and turned a corner. He was jealous of the man, who had got Miss Carol's attention.

Anu was afraid to ask where she was, in case the other children would jeer him for having a crush on her. Tomorrow he would ask one of the other teachers if she had left the school to go back to Canada.

Across the street he noticed a man watching him. The man remained there as the tuk-tuks and cars drove past. When he looked again, he noticed the man crossing the street towards the shop. Anu wished his mother was with him at this time. The man moved slowly towards him, bushy eyebrows knitted together as he glared through Anu's skull. *Was he casting an evil eye?*

The man came in and nodded to him. He picked up one of the painted wooden dolls and pretended to be interested in it, even though he was a local. Anu noticed that he was watching him from the corner of his eye. A smell of stale sweat and raw onions permeated the store.

"Thirty baht." He hoped the stranger did not detect fear in his tone.

The customer ignored him. The man looked closely at the doll saying nothing, slowly turning it in his hand. Anu hoped another customer would show up soon. The man put down the doll.

"You go to school?"

"Yes."

"Good. Young boys should go to school. Learn something. Maybe you will get a good job after you finish school."

Anu said nothing.

"Which school?"

"St. Cecilia's."

"Oh? I know a *farang* teacher there." *Farang.* He hated that word. It meant a Westerner in Thai. The bullies sometimes called him *Farangi bastard.*

Anu did not take the bait for further conversation.

"The doll. You can have it. Twenty Baht." He dusted off some of the souvenirs.

The man came nearer to him. His body odour was overpowering. He lowered his voice. "You like your teacher, don't you?"

How did this man know about his secret passion for Carol? Could he really see into his brain with those piercing eyes?

"Ten baht. Take the doll please."

The man shook his head.

A couple of tourists entered the shop. The man quickly turned and left.

Who was that man? What did he want? Why did he ask about Miss Carol?

Chapter 9

"I know what happened Carol. You better come Bangkok soon." The note had been handwritten.

Jessica took the crow and put it in the grass in the back alley. She had read somewhere that crows had emotions and others would show up when one of theirs had died. She recalled that a dead crow may mean more death, or good fortune. This was a message for her. It was an invitation to Bangkok. A grotesque one. But she knew she had to go there even if this was a trap. She had to find Carol and deal with the bastards who had kidnapped her. They were trying to scare her into coming. Expecting that she would timidly arrive and play into their hands. They were in for a big surprise. Bastards. How dare they touch Carol! This had to be a kidnapping. Sending Jariya to her was the start. The dead crow was meant to terrify her but it had the opposite effect. She was more determined now. In a way she found this encouraging. It meant that Carol was alive. Why else would she be told to come to Bangkok now? She must act fast.

She ran up the stairs and checked all the rooms to make sure nobody had broken in and taken anything. All was in order. There was no sign that anyone had been in the house.

There was no time to waste. She had to talk to Karen in person. Nearing Karen's house in the Parkdale district, she stopped as a black cat crossed the street. It used the pedestrian crosswalk. *How odd* she thought. She had seen deer do that in one of the small towns south of Calgary. The cat stopped and looked at her and then continued on. *This can't be happening. It's trying to tell me something. Nonsense! I am not superstitious like my mother was.*

She gunned her Buick down Crowchild Trail. A biker gave her the finger for cutting him off. She ignored him and sped along. She hoped a radar trap would not be at the usual spot when she turned off onto 14th street. There wasn't. There was no time to lose.

Jessica rang the doorbell. No answer. She knocked loudly. Finally, she heard someone behind the door.

"Jess! Sorry, I just had the hair dryer on. Come in." Karen smoothed her hair into place.

They sat together on the chesterfield.

"Do you want some tea?"

"No, thanks. No time for that."

"What's wrong? Your face is flushed. Did you have an accident?"

Quietly Jessica told her everything that had happened. She also told her about the meeting with Len.

Karen held her head in her hands, trying to make sense of what she had just been told by her closest friend. She knew Jessica had a drinking problem but there was no smell of alcohol on her breath and she believed she was getting out of the habit. She put her arm around her and took her into the den. Dr. Phil was giving his advice to a quarrelling couple. Karen turned the TV set off.

"Oh Jessica, this is so horrible! It's like a nightmare. What are we going to do? We don't know anyone in Bangkok."

"It doesn't matter. I have to go there. The sooner the better."

"I'll come with you." Karen had stayed close to Jessica since Carol had left. "But first let me check if my passport is still valid," said Karen. She went to the upstairs bedroom to check and returned with her laptop and passport in hand. "Yes, it's still got another year on it. Count me in."

She checked flight schedules. "There's an Air Canada flight tomorrow to Vancouver connecting in Tokyo and then Bangkok."

"Let's book it for both of us. Here's my credit card," said Jessica as she passed it to her. Karen's ex had been a big spender and left her with little in the way of funds. Her work as a physiotherapist did not provide enough money for her mortgage and living expenses.

"OK, thanks. Let me call Dave to look after my place and yours while we are away. This may be short notice for him but he would never turn down his good old mum. His dad, maybe but not me." After Karen's divorce she often sought help from her son, who also looked on Jessica as an aunt. 'Auntie Jessie', he would teasingly call her.

"I'll make the booking now. Why don't you go home and pack? I'll come later and spend the night with you. "I'll call a cab to pick us up from your place in the morning."

"Thanks. See you soon."

Back at home, Jessica's first check was the computer. The screen came to life as she touched the keyboard. A quick check of emails. Nothing from Carol, only one from Len.

'Jessica, I emailed my friend Pattama in Bangkok. Am waiting to hear from him. Will keep you informed. Good luck and keep the faith! Sincerely, Len.'

'Thanks Len,' she wrote back *'will be leaving on the earliest flight possible. Will let you know which hotel we will be staying at. Karen Delaney will be my travelling companion. She is a friend of many years."*

She hurried off an email to Karen to tell her that Len had lined up some local assistance in Bangkok.

Jessica remembered something. After she had discovered the crow, she had not looked in the dresser and closet in Carol's room. Could someone have entered her room, or just left the crow in the mailbox? It was time to check.

Going upstairs now seemed more strenuous. She used to take two steps at a time but alcohol had been slowing her down in the last two years.

It's just me being silly. Why would someone go into Carol's room? Surely the crow in the mailbox was enough! Her breath was stuck in her throat. No air was going into her lungs as she carefully opened Carol's door. The bed was undisturbed. The framed photo of Ben, Carol and her together at the beach was still in place. *She should have taken that picture with her. But then, she was going away to forget...*

Opening her clothes closet, most of the clothes were gone, packed in the suitcase she had taken with her. She pushed the bifold door closed and heard something drop in the closet. She opened it again. A paper bag had fallen from the closet shelf. The contents, brochures of Thailand, had spilled out. Carol had probably got these after her visit to the Thai Consulate. There was however a newspaper clipping that was not likely from the Consulate. It was an article in the Calgary Today newspaper entitled *'Sex Tourism in Thailand. What you need to know.'*

Jessica scanned the article quickly. *Had she intended to help some locals to get out of this way of life and got punished for it? She was, after all, a young idealistic girl who wanted to change the world. But had she paid the price?*

Jessica stuffed the clipping back into the bag and gently closed the closet door.

Chapter 10

There had been flight delays due to a spring snowstorm in Toronto which backed up most of the domestic flights. Angry and tired passengers packed the departure lounge. There were only three passengers in line for First-Class. One, a bejeweled older lady, looked condescendingly at the large line-up and shook her head. "Poor children. Their parents should have been prepared for this," she murmured.

Her husband nodded in agreement, buttoned up his blue blazer before approaching the agent who checked them in. The agent signalled to Jessica to come forward and took her ticket.

"Our Vancouver connection is on time, Mrs. Guthrie. I see you are going to Bangkok. Are you two ladies travelling together?" she asked as she looked at Karen.

"Yes, we are. How long is the stop at Narita airport?" asked Jessica.

"Four hours, but it will be the same Air Canada plane you will be re-boarding to Bangkok. Is it your first visit to Thailand?"

"Yes," Jessica put her passport into her handbag.

The agent printed their boarding passes and tagged their bags which were on the conveyor belt. "Have a nice trip."

'Sure,' Jessica thought, '*this is going to be a great trip.*'

They were flying over the mountains. Blankets of snow still clung to the higher peaks despite the warm spring weather.

"There won't be any snow in Bangkok that's for sure," said Jessica. She took out her new cellphone which she had purchased a few weeks ago. It was important to check all the new features since this would be her lifeline in Bangkok. It had a good Display and the photos that she had taken in Calgary were very clear and sharp. Ben and Carol had shown her how useful a cellphone could be, especially in an emergency.

The hour passed quickly. The plane made a wide loop over the ocean and came in for the landing at Vancouver International Airport.

"Should we have a quick snack here before we board the next flight?"

"Why? Won't they give us a good meal on the plane?" asked Jessica.

"They will, but it may not be anything you like. They don't serve donuts in First-Class. I want a *Tim Hortons* donut. Need the sugar rush before the flight."

Not long after the donut fix at *Tim Hortons,* they began boarding for the flight to Tokyo's Narita airport. The First-Class cabin had only four other passengers in the ten-seat cabin. Three Japanese businessmen returning to Tokyo politely bowed to them, the only women in Business Class. A swarthy person in a well tailored dark suit, who could have been a Middle Eastern businessman, sat across the aisle from Karen. He smiled and nodded to them.

The engines whined and the plane began to taxi towards the runaway.

"Welcome aboard! I am First Officer Sims. Our flight time to Narita airport in Tokyo will be nine hours and fifteen minutes. The weather is very pleasant there, not like it was in Toronto."

The plane gathered speed on the runaway and was soon airborne. Vancouver's lights twinkled as the plane gained altitude before they shot through a cloud bank and leveled off. Seat belt lights turned off and then a flight attendant hovered over them. "Some champagne?"

"Please."

Jessica sipped her glass. "Something does not fit."

"What are you talking about?" asked Karen.

"Jariya Panya. She was on the level. I felt it. She was very sweet."

"Maybe she was just a good actor."

"I don't think so. She would not have planted the dead crow there. She did not seem the type of person who would do such a nasty thing. She would not hurt any bird, far too timid. I feel that there was a man behind this. He likely forced her to come with him from Bangkok and convince me."

"So, what happened to Carol?"

"Not sure, but probably kidnapped. I believe that Jariya Panya was recruited unknowingly by whoever kidnapped her."

"Seems like a complicated way to get ransom money. How did they find Jariya?"

"It's not difficult. Finding someone to travel to a rich country is easy. So, the kidnappers get Carol's photo from her apartment. They approach Jariya and offer to send her to Canada to convince me. A ruse to lure me here."

"But why?"

"They expect I will be more vulnerable in Bangkok. They are correct. Bastards!"

"Didn't you say that Len was going to have someone meet you at the airport?"

"Yes, and the kidnappers will probably know that I will have a local person helping out."

"Interesting."

"Menus?" The stewardess handed them the embossed pamphlets.

Filet Mignon with baked potato
Grilled Salmon with steamed asparagus
Roasted Vegetables with Camembert and Blue Cheese.

"No red meat for me," said Jessica.

"What about the salmon?" Karen recalled her fine salmon dinner when she had been visiting Tofino in British Columbia.

"I'll go with the Roasted Vegetables."

"Becoming a vegetarian, are you Jessica?"

"Not yet, but I'm considering it."

"Supposed to be healthy. The doctors on TV keep pushing for us to eat more fruit and vegetables. I think I'll always be a carnivore," said Karen.

An infant started to cry in the Economy section. It did not seem that long ago that Carol was in her crib, crying to be picked up and fed. Now she was holed up somewhere in Bangkok waiting for Jessica to help her again.

"Did you know that Thailand used to be called Siam?" asked Jessica.

"Wish Yul Brynner was still around. He could have helped get me out of this mess."

"And when he is done, maybe we can whistle a happy tune as Deborah Kerr did in that movie." Jessica took a sip of her champagne. She had to take care not to drink too much on the aircraft

49

since she knew that alcohol got to you faster in flight. She put the glass aside.

"Not the right type of Champagne?" asked the Middle Eastern gentleman.

"Don't feel like it," muttered Jessica trying not to be too friendly as she saw the man take a quick glance at her legs.

"Where will you stay in Tokyo?" His accent was British. Probably educated in a fine college in the UK.

"Won't be. Going somewhere else."

"Ooh, too bad. Tokyo is a beautiful city. Should stay at least few days."

Sure. And be escorted by you, no doubt!

He reached into his coat jacket and gave her his card. She didn't glance at it but left it on the arm of the seat.

"Please call, if you do stay in Tokyo. I can take you to some nice restaurants and places to shop."

Karen smiled politely.

"As I was saying..." said Jessica, as she frowned at the man who smiled, nodded and looked straight ahead. He got the message.

"They still have a King you know," said Karen.

Jessica opened the Air Canada magazine and looked at the world map.

"I know very little about Thailand. Only that they have a good tourist trade."

"They also have a very lucrative sex trade."

"The dark side of the tourist business."
Jessica flipped through the pages.

"Speaking about dark, maybe we should get some sleep. We have a long, long journey ahead of us." Karen put on the sleeping mask and fully reclined her seat.

"I'm not sleepy yet. Need to watch some dumb movies before I sleep."

She looked at the movie menu and selected *Up in the Air*, since she liked George Clooney. For this trip she would have preferred Bruce Willis as an additional companion.

It's going to be hot in Thailand, not just the temperature, she thought. *How should she react when the kidnappers got in touch with her? She was sure it would be within the first week. Should she get a gun? Guns are probably legal in Thailand. She would have to have lessons though, since she had never used one.*

The hum of the engines and low light in the cabin helped her doze off. Sleep was what she needed now.

Karen nudged Jessica to wake her up.

"We've arrived in Tokyo. Need to get off since there is a four-hour layover."

They gathered their carry-on luggage. The Middle Eastern gentleman smiled at Jessica again as he put on his jacket.

"I could not help overhearing that you are going on to Bangkok. It's a very nice city on the surface. But be careful. Be very careful."

He turned and left the aircraft before Jessica could say anything.

Chapter 11

Len was not having a good day at the office. His new boss, Ed, continued to pressure him, and the other staff and it was likely his first managerial position. His behaviour was obnoxious and often Len came close to cursing him.

"Len, have you read the damage report I gave to you this morning?"

"Not yet, Ed. I am reviewing the file on the Wilson case," he answered.

"Forget about the Wilson case, Len! We are not paying him a cent and our contract is very clear related to Force Majeure."

"OK, I'll drop it and review the damage report for the Coburns."

Len bristled. *This fucking asshole. How dare he push me around like this! He was in diapers when I completed my fourth year at U. of T.*

He stood up, opened the file cabinet drawer, fished out the Coburn case, and slammed the drawer shut. Ed raised his eyebrows but said nothing.

Len looked at the first page but his mind was elsewhere. By now Jessica Guthrie must be in Bangkok. He had alerted his former colleague about Jessica's arrival time. He had not received a response from Pattama to the email he had sent him. However, 'Pat' as Len called him, had proved to be a dependable person. He could not wait to get home and call Pat. It was important that Jessica be met at the airport and feel comfortable with him. He was a charming person, especially with ladies. Len felt that Jessica would take to him.

"Len, can you come to my office right away?" Ed barked.

"Yes, will be there in a moment, Ed."

He quickly scanned the three pages of the report to see if anything jumped out at him that he needed to discuss with Ed. This job was getting to him. It was dull and boring. So, unlike a field position where the pounding of piles and pouring of concrete was his passion, he had to tolerate this low-paying work in an office that was more lifeless than a funeral home. He had tried for two years to find a senior position with an Engineering company but had no success. To make ends meet he had to take this Insurance Adjuster's job. He hated it, but it paid his rent and groceries. The salary was a quarter of what he got when he was with Guthrie Construction.

He hurried over to Ed's office.

"Close the door please Len, and take a seat."

Len did not like the tone of voice and shifted uncomfortably in his chair.

"Len, how do you like your job?"

"It's great, Ed. A bit different from my previous field of work, but interesting nonetheless."

"Well, since I took over the department last month, I have been evaluating all of you."

"Oh, that's good, got to get to know us all," said Len.

"Len, I don't think you are a good fit for the Insurance business and I am letting you go."

"What? Pardon?"

Len was stunned. This had never happened to him before. He was always a good performer. His blood was rising but he held his temper in check.

"You heard me, Len. Friday will be your last day. I will pay you for another two weeks, which is in compliance with our employment contract."

Len felt tempted to rip up the report in his hand and fling the pieces at Ed. His professionalism stopped him from doing this. Instead, he turned and left the room without saying another word to Ed. It was only Tuesday but he had no intention to work until Friday and he would leave immediately. He removed his desk set, given to him by Ben Guthrie, and the photograph of him and Ben at their last jobsite. He closed the desk drawer and

55

stalked out of the office while Ed followed behind him.

"Len! Come back here!" Ed yelled.

Fuck you, you son of a bitch, he thought as he slammed the office door.

His eyes closed to adjust to the strong sunlight in the parking lot. He had far more important matters to attend to than this shit-ass job. Ed could shove the two-weeks pay up his ass.

Chapter 12

"One of your teachers came by today," said Anu's mother as she dusted their sparse furniture.

"What did she want?"

"It was a man. He said he teaches you sports at the school and wanted to let you know about an upcoming football game."

"I don't have a male teacher who teaches us sports. What did the man look like?"

"Not too tall. Seemed a bit shy. Smelled like a dead rat," Taneka answered.

Anu froze. This must be the same person who had come to the shop. He told his mother of the stranger's visit. Her heart pounded and her temples throbbed. But she did not want to show Anu that she was afraid. She knew kidnapping was a lively trade in some countries but had thought that Thailand was relatively safe, especially Bangkok. But the city had changed a lot since she was a child.

"Anu, I need to get you your own cellphone." She hoped he did not sense the fear in her voice.

Anu was all she had. She loved him more than anyone else she had known, including her own parents.

Anu had always wanted a cellphone. However, this was not a gift but an important link to his mother if he was in danger. She had her own cellphone which they had shared. Although he was afraid of the stranger, he thought that perhaps his mother was overreacting.

"I'll be fine, Mum. Please use the money for something else you need."

"No, Anu. I will get you one tomorrow. Promise me that you will call me if you see this man again. You know that some bad things have happened in the city."

Anu did not think Bangkok was dangerous. It was a lively place and sure, there were red-light areas to avoid where the pimps hung out with their girls to lure in the tourists. He had often walked alone and had never felt threatened. What could this man do to him, in broad daylight? He had not looked very strong and Anu had seen movies of smaller men knocking out bigger bullies. He felt he could handle this man since his mother kept a baseball bat behind the cash register for her protection.

"OK, Mum, if it makes you feel better, please get me one, but not an iPhone. They are too expensive."

His mother kept on dusting and hoped that Anu wouldn't notice her trembling fingers. *This had never happened before. How dare this man come to their home!*

She did not trust the police who ignored local poorer folk and only paid attention to the rich people and tourists. She remembered their condescending attitude when she had tried to track down Anu's father. They had treated her like a prostitute and she would never forget that. How things had changed over the years. Bangkok had been so safe when she was a child. She could go anywhere and not feel threatened. All that had changed due to the curse of the Tourist industry where sex was a big tourist attraction. The Viet Nam war had also brought in many American servicemen. She was ashamed that her countrymen had sacrificed their traditions and moral upbringing. But then, she had made mistakes too, when she needed money to fend off starvation. She would never tell Anu that.

"Mama, why did the man ask me about Miss Carol?"

"Maybe he was trying to make friends with you."

"Did I tell you that she has not been in school for the last few days?"

"No, you didn't."

"I saw her going away with another man after school last week. I did not see her again after that."

"Would the man be the stranger who visited you?"

Anu tried to recollect the scene. He had only seen an older man go around the corner with Miss Carol. There may have been others around the corner or elsewhere, but he could not recall seeing the stranger at the scene. Perhaps one of them was on the street and saw Miss Carol leave with the other man. Maybe that was the man who came to the shop.

"I am afraid, Mama."

"Don't be afraid son. You will not be alone." Taneka said nothing more. She herself was street-smart but could not handle harm coming to her only child.

"No, I am not afraid for myself. I am afraid for Miss Carol."

"What do you mean?"

"I think she may have been kidnapped. That man probably led her to others."

"Well, her parents will make a report to the police. They will act on it right away since they are probably wealthy westerners who are living in Thailand now."

"No, she is in Bangkok alone. She told us that she only has a mother in Canada. Her father died a few years ago."

"Well, maybe the school will do something. It is not our business." Taneka did not want to involve her son in what may be a sex-trade kidnapping. But she was worried for the poor girl and wished that she could do something to help. The system was so unjust for women.

Anu was silent. He would tell the Principal tomorrow that he had seen Miss Carol leaving the school with another man. Perhaps the Principal will tell him that she was on a holiday and had not 'just disappeared'. His gut feeling was otherwise. Miss Carol was in danger. He must do all he can to help find her.

His noble intentions would get him into serious trouble.

Chapter 13

"That man gave me the creeps, even though he looked like Omar Sharif. He seems to be an experienced traveler though, and must have been in Bangkok to give me that 'heads up'."

"Beware of tall, dark, handsome strangers," Karen said.

They were boarding for the trip to Bangkok. New passengers in the First-Class cabin included two westerners. The rest were Asian businessmen. One of the westerners wore an Astros baseball cap. He looked at them and smiled.

"Long way from home, ladies!" His Houston accent came through loud and clear. "First trip to Bangkok?"

"No, we will be meeting our husbands there," volunteered Jessica before Karen could speak. This brought the exchange of pleasantries to a quick end. They reclined their seats after the plane reached cruising altitude. Shortly after their meal, they fell asleep.

"Good morning! This is your captain speaking. We will be landing in Bangkok in thirty minutes." He droned on with the usual thanks to customers for using the airline.

Jessica shook Karen, who was still asleep.

"Wake up! We'll be landing soon."

"Where are we?" Karen was still groggy.

"Almost in Bangkok."

"Already? You mean I slept for so long?"

"Hard to believe so much time in the air can make you tired."

The Air Canada pilot and crew smiled to them as they exited the aircraft. "Thank you for flying with us. Enjoy your stay in Bangkok."

Sure, thought Jessica, *nothing could be more enjoyable than searching for your missing daughter in a strange city.*

The Thai Customs official took a brief glance at their passports and waved them through without smiling.

"Good God! Have you ever seen such a beautiful airport?" The terminal included several gold-painted figures in traditional warrior poses. Gleaming replicas of pagodas were in some parts of the terminal. Sunlight gave the roof a diaphanous glow and the tiled floor was spotless.

"Calgary International looks like a dump compared to this," Karen exclaimed.

"There must be a better word to describe this than 'spectacular'," said Jessica. "I remember

Carol telling me that she was blown away by this when she first arrived."

They picked up their baggage from the carousel. Hundreds of passengers milled around and looked for their tour guides, friends or relatives. Some of them appeared to be expats who knew their way around. Jessica and Karen stopped at an Information Desk.

"Excuse me. We need to get a taxi to the Metropole Hotel."

"Taxi? Please go exit thirty-nine. All taxis and hotel buses standing there. Thank you. Welcome to Thailand!"

They were hit by a wave of hot, humid air as they left the terminal building.

"Good God! This is like a sauna!"

"Get used to it, Karen. We could be here for awhile." They squinted in the bright sunlight looking for the bus stop.

"Which hotel, Missus?" The taxi driver asked as he took their bags and loaded it into the trunk. He nodded when Jessica told him The Metropole.

"This is quite the city. I would never have thought it was so modern," remarked Karen.

"I have read that it is a very historic city and that improvements are made regularly to roads, bridges and the water system. Since tourism generates a lot of revenue for Thailand, this is critical to them," said Jessica.

"Have you ever seen such beautiful trees and flowers?"

"You cannot compare our home city to this place. They get lots of rain during the monsoon season and just about everything grows. However, expect insects, bugs and snakes as part of Mother Nature's down side."

Some poorer areas could be seen as they drove toward the hotel. In the distance were tall buildings which could have been the commercial area of Bangkok. They arrived at *The Metropole Hotel* in the centre of a lush garden with palm trees, manicured lawns and bushes with flowers in full bloom. The taxi driver stopped and opened the door for them.

"Thank you," said Jessica as she gave him her credit card.

"Cash only, please. US dollars or baht." Jessica gave him twenty US dollars which made him spring into action to take out their luggage from the trunk.

"Hope you like Bangkok. Here my card if you need taxi today, tomorrow. Thank you, thank you." He bowed and smiled.

"I wish we had such beautiful gardens outside our hotels in Calgary," marveled Karen.

The hotel attendant took their luggage and led them to the Front Desk. The Front Desk Clerk had been sizing them up from the moment they exited the cab.

Couple of American women who left their husbands home to sample the locals. No, maybe their husbands are here on business and will meet them here soon. Not too bad looking, the two of them. I could entertain them both, preferably one at a time of course. Maybe they are British. Been seeing a lot of them since the Pound is doing well. That's my guess: British! From London. Left the cold dreary streets to get some sun.

He looked up and smiled broadly. "Reservations?"

"Yes. Jessica Guthrie and Karen Delaney. From Canada."

"Passports please." *Shit I was wrong. Canadians!*

"Why do you need our passports?"

His broad smile hid his thoughts. *Never been outside North America I'll bet. If they had been traveling in Europe or Asia, they would have known this is normal practice.*

"We need to verify your identity for your protection, Mrs. Guthrie. Hotel policy. So sorry. Many hotels in countries outside Canada ask for passports. Please?"

Jessica looked at Karen, shook her head and handed it to the clerk who took a cursory look at hers and handed it back.

"Thank you, Mrs. Guthrie. Will you use your Visa card for the final bill, or would you like to change to another?"

"No change. Stay with Visa."

He keyed in her information on a machine which programmed her room cardkey.

"This is the card for Room 512, and another card for Mrs. Delaney's room, 514. She is next door to you. Also, there is a letter for you, Mrs. Guthrie. I will get it now."

"Can you please give me a city map too?"

The clerk nodded, gave her a map from under the desk and went into the office. He returned with an envelope and gave it to Jessica.

"Enjoy your stay. I will have someone help you with your bags." He rang for the bellhop who appeared immediately.

"Thank you." She took the envelope and followed the bellhop to the elevator. As they waited, she opened the envelope to reveal a neat handwritten note:

Dear Mrs. Guthrie,

My friend Len Green has asked me to assist you with regards to locating your daughter. Please call me whenever you wish, at 02-444-9966.

Sincerely,

Pattama (Pat)

The bellhop opened their room doors and stood politely as Jessica and Karen fumbled in their purses for a tip.

"I'll call him from the phone in my room right now," Karen offered.

Jessica waited as she dialed.

"Oops, his line is busy. Hello this is Karen Delaney, Jessica Guthrie's travelling companion. Thank you for your note. Can you meet us in the hotel tomorrow morning at 10.00 a.m.? Look forward to seeing you Pat."

"I am so tired..."

"Me too," yawned Jessica "best to get lots of sleep before we shake up the town tomorrow."

"Bangkok will likely shake us up! Never been to a place like this. So many people. So much traffic. Knock on my door tomorrow morning if I'm not awake by nine."

"Have a good night..." Karen gently closed the door behind her while Jessica unplugged the phone from the wall outlet. She wanted to get well rested for the exhausting day ahead. A clear head was necessary to confront the adversity that lay ahead. *If it's only money they want, I have it.*

The room was one of the better ones she had stayed at. *Thais liked to put lots of colour in their surroundings. Probably want their rooms to look like a flower garden too.* She opened her suitcase and took out her toiletries and put them next to the sink on the white marble vanity with polished brass taps. The mirror over the sink was not the utilitarian type in Canadian hotels. The frame itself was worthy of having a painting in it. It was exquisitely carved wood, possibly teak inlaid with onyx. She looked at herself in the mirror. Eyes were red, due to lack of sleep. *Better get some sleep soon* she thought as she removed her clothes and slipped on her nightdress.

Jessica turned off the light and lay on the large comfortable bed. Such a long way from home. Carol was indeed a brave girl to participate in these adventures. But then again, India had been her first trip and she probably found this far less adventurous. She had never been afraid in Bangalore. Many friendly people and kind souls who helped her to get to know their local customs. In her early emails she had mentioned that Bangkok was too fast paced and commercialized as compared to Bangalore. It was far more crowded than any other city she had been to. Fatigue soon put thoughts of Carol in the background as she slipped into her dreams in Thailand.

But her nightmares were to begin the next day.

Chapter 14

"Mrs. Guthrie, so pleased to meet you."

Jessica was pleasantly surprised. She expected to meet a shy person, similar to his friend Len. Instead Pattama was very different. Tall, athletic build and very charming. She could see that Karen was flustered as she patted her hair to ensure no strands were out of place for this gorgeous man.

"Jessica, please."

"And this must be Mrs. Delaney?"

"Karen."

"Karen, I'm Pattama, please call me Pat." He shook her hand and Jessica could see a blush. She was obviously smitten.

"Hello. Nice to meet you," blurted Karen.

"Have you had breakfast yet?" asked Pat.

"No, we were waiting for you. We can go to the restaurant in the hotel," suggested Jessica.

"I have a better idea. There is a nice place down the road. A better atmosphere for you lovely ladies."

Pat ushered them to his car which was parked at the entrance. It was a late model, dark blue Mustang. *The car suits the man. Young and sleek.* Karen thought. A short drive down a tropical boulevard led them to a restaurant by the river.

"Hello Pattama," said the hostess, a slim, attractive Thai lady. She spoke English mindful of his company.

"Hi, Lallana! Can you find us a nice quiet table for the ladies and me?"

The tables were set against the large glass windows which overlooked the Chao Praya river, which snaked through the tropical trees and meandered towards the modern office buildings in the heart of the city.

"Ladies, please." Pat gestured for them to take the chairs by the window. He sat next to Karen.

A waitress poured mango juice into the crystal glasses on their table and left them the breakfast menu. Pat's smile faded as he looked at Jessica.

"I'm so sorry to hear that your first visit to this beautiful city is not a holiday. I promise that I will do all I can to assist. Len sent me Carol's photos and I have already done some digging."

"Oh. Any early results?" asked Jessica.

"No leads yet. You do know however that Bangkok can be dangerous for unaccompanied young girls."

"Yes, I am aware of that."

"When did you last hear from Carol?"

"More than a week ago, an email. She wrote at least a couple a week. Then, nothing..."

Pat gestured to the waitress. He spoke in Thai and she nodded and went away.

"I have ordered some fresh fruit for starters. I am certain you will love custard apple, jackfruit and guava."

"I love guava. Never had custard apple or jackfruit before," said Karen as she sipped her mango juice.

Pat touched her hand. "I guarantee you will enjoy them both."

His expression became serious again. "We don't have much time and must act fast. I know a sergeant in the local police. He told me that there have been six kidnappings of Western girls within the last month. This is unusual for Bangkok."

"But Carol was always very careful and quite street-smart!"

"Being street-smart in Canada versus this part of the world is quite different. There are some young hippies who come here fully trusting the locals. Unfortunately, there are some well-organized criminal gangs. They pose as security officers but they are really just pimps. They ship the girls off to be concubines in Middle Eastern countries where they have no rights."

Jessica froze. *Was this what may have happened to her?*

"But Carol had a full-time job in a school and did not live very far away from it."

"Doesn't matter. I'm sure she went out to the local clubs. Most young people do and they seldom tell their parents about these places."

Jessica remembered the close call Carol had in India, when a man posing as a police officer wanted her to open the door to her apartment. She was smart enough not to. It was not likely that she had been conned into something. They must have forcibly put her in a car and driven off. *Oh, God. I need your help!*

Chapter 15

Anu took his time walking to school. He was lost in thought. Asking to speak to the Principal was not normally done unless there was an emergency of some type. How would he do this? Should he just walk over to the office and ask to see him? The office staff would probably tell him to go away or will ask him why he needed to see the principal. He had not previously spoken to him and had seen him only at assembly. He was a stern man, not someone to be trifled with. Playing out in his mind what he should say, he was soon at the school gate. The class would start in fifteen minutes. *Should he go to the office now, or should he wait until after school? After school would be better.* He would need more time to think.

The bell rang and the students entered their classrooms. Anu sat down, opened his school bag and took out his exercise book to the page on which he had done his homework. The new teacher walked in and introduced herself. She was a Thai native and she enunciated her English words incorrectly. Her style was very different from Miss Carol's who had been less strict and more attentive to a student's needs. He found it hard to concentrate on the first lesson in Arithmetic. He was not good at it and his mind was elsewhere in a prison where Miss Carol was likely being held. He could not wait for the school day to end.

When the class was over, he walked over to the teacher's desk.

"Excuse me, Miss."

"Yes, what do you want?"

"Has Miss Carol gone back to Canada?"

"I do not know. That will be all. You should go now."

There was no point in pursuing this further with her, so he left the class and began to walk to the Principal's office.

"May I see Mr. Suttikul?"

"What is your name young man?"

"Anurak Montri."

"You do not have an appointment. Mr. Suttikul is a very busy man."

"But..."

"Young man, go away. I told you that our Principal is a busy man. Ask your parents to contact our office and we will make an appointment for them." The woman turned away and walked back to her desk, ignoring Anu, who waited a few more moments before leaving the office.

He did not go home but waited in the schoolyard and kept a close watch on the main school door. Most of the staff had left but he had not seen the principal leave. He waited patiently. The door opened and Mr. Suttikul came down the steps holding the railing with one hand while the other carried his satchel. Anu moved quickly towards him.

"Sir. I have some important information for you."

The principal looked at him and his face appeared to soften. This young man had some courage he thought, to approach him like that.

"What is your name?"

"Anurak Montri, sir."

"And what have you to tell me? Complaints about teachers?"

"No, sir. It's about Miss Carol."

"Was she your teacher?"

"Yes, sir. I think she is in trouble."

The Principal stiffened. "What kind of trouble? Boyfriend problems?"

"No, sir. After school last week, I saw a man approach her. He spoke to her animatedly and then she went with him around a corner."

"Oh? Did he have a car?"

"I don't know but he led her around a corner and there may have been one there. Perhaps there were others. She did not come to school the next day. That would have been last Tuesday."

"Come to my office young man. I need to make some notes. Her mother has an appointment with me tomorrow morning."

He followed the principal into his office. They were alone, all the staff had left. An unusual period of silence in this noisy school.

"Sit down, Mr. Montri." The principal gestured to one of the chairs in front of his desk. The man was well-organized and the only items on the desk were a notepad and his pen set. A photograph on the wall behind him showed him shaking hands with the superintendent of schools who appeared to be presenting him with some sort of award plaque.

Anu sat on the edge of the chair, and tried not to look too comfortable. He was pleased that the Principal called him Mr. Montri and not Anu. No one else had called him 'Mr. Montri'.

The principal took his pen and began to write on the pad. "These young foreign girls sometimes go to the wrong places in this city. You know there are some bad areas in Bangkok, don't you, young man?"

"Yes, sir. But Miss Carol was different. She told us she did not like going to bars, or going dancing. She is here because she wants to help young Thai students."

"They all say that. Tell me what time you saw her and give me a description of the man. Did he have glasses? What type of clothes or shoes? Have you seen him near the school before?"

The principal scribbled notes while Anu recounted what he had seen. After he was done, the Principal told him that he may need to see him again in the morning when Carol's mother was to visit.

Anu left the office, very pleased with what he had done. He was also happy that Miss Carol's mother was in Bangkok and that he would meet her.

He opened the school gate and turned left to go to his home. He froze. The stranger was there again, but this time there was another man with him. Anu turned and ran. He could hear them running after him shouting for him to stop. He didn't. He turned into an alley and ran across the street dodging rickshaws, tuk-tuks and motorists who blew their horns at him. He hid behind a tree to see if he had lost them. There was no sign of them. He would have to be very careful when he came to the street where he lived. He knew they would be waiting for him.

He wished he had got the cellphone sooner. It would have been so useful now. He made his way to his street, looking all around him. It was not a busy street and off the main road near the railroad tracks. Anu saw the large palm tree and bougainvillea bush that was near their hut in the shanty town. He broke into a run and dashed into the hut. Two men were already in his home. His mother was tied with rope to a chair and had a gag on her mouth. She squirmed when she saw him and tried to say something. Her wide eyes were imploring him to run away.

"Hello Anu." It was the man who had visited the shop. The men smiled and showed his yellow teeth. His friend, a younger, muscular man, held a knife in one hand and his mother's hair in the other.

"You will come with me now. My friend will remain with your mother until I call him. If you make any attempt to run away from me, or call for help, your mother will pay."

Taneka struggled and tried to dislodge the gag from her mouth. She was not able to move and the other man held her and kept the gag in place over her mouth. Anu lunged towards her but he was grabbed by the neck and dragged to the corner of the room.

"I told you. No screaming! Or else your mother will regret it, and so will you." He nodded to the other man who held the knife to Taneka's throat.

"You will come with me now! Behave yourself on the street or your mother will be killed and it will be your fault." He grabbed Anu's hand and held it firmly.

"We will walk like father and son on the street. A tuk-tuk will be here soon."

Anu was helpless.

"Mama, I will be back soon, don't worry."

The two men smiled. "Yes, don't worry. Your son is in good hands."

Chapter 16

Jessica and Karen took a taxi to Carol's school. The principal was pleased to have a North American visitor. It sometimes meant a donation to the school but in this case, he did not expect one. The secretary brought them a steaming pot of jasmine tea and poured it into small earthenware cups on a brass tray. He rose to greet his guest. "Good morning, Mrs. Guthrie and ..."

"Good morning. This is my friend Karen Delaney from Canada." Jessica and Karen shook his hand, sat down and took the cups of tea offered by the secretary.

The principal took his seat. "I am so sorry for our missing Carol and I will give you whatever help you need. I'm sure this is very difficult for you but we can all hope that she has not been harmed. It's just been a few days since she hasn't been at school. When did you last speak to Carol?"

"We exchanged emails on a regular basis and there was no cause for alarm. She really liked it here in Bangkok and spoke highly of her students

81

and your school. Not once did she mention anything negative about the city or her circumstances." Jessica did not want to reveal to him that she had a strange visitor in Calgary.

"That is good to hear. Bangkok is a popular city but is generally safe. There are of course some local miscreants who take advantage of tourists but it is mainly pickpockets and other petty crimes. I have not heard of any tourists being kidnapped in Bangkok. Are you sure she has not gone hiking with friends without telling you? Sometimes young people do that."

"We exchange emails regularly. If she intended to go anywhere out of Bangkok, she would have told me. Carol is quite mature and would not take unnecessary risks."

"Yes, I have known Carol since she was a baby. She is a very cautious girl and is very close to her mother." Karen sighed and sipped her cup of tea.

"Umm, let me send for one of the students who saw her before she went missing. Mrs. Willapana! Please send for Mr. Montri!"

"Yes, sir." The secretary who had shown them in, left the office to summon Anu from the class.

"Mrs. Guthrie, your daughter was very popular with the students, even though she had little previous experience with teaching."

"Carol is an optimistic young woman and loves working with children. She volunteered at an orphanage in India. I'm sure her enthusiasm came through to the students."

Mrs. Willapana opened the door after a gentle knock. "Mr. Montri is not in the class today. He had no absences until today. We have not heard from him, or his mother."

"Oh, perhaps both of them are ill today. Mrs. Guthrie, maybe we can arrange for you to meet with him at the hotel. When he comes in tomorrow, we will ask him to contact you. In the meantime, I will meet with each of my staff to ask if there are any clues as to where Carol may be. Perhaps she has confided with one of her friends. Sometimes daughters do not tell their parents about romantic interests. I hope that this is the case. I will let you know as soon as I hear anything. But rest assured, we are all praying for her safety."

"Thank you, Mr. Suttikul." They finished their tea, exchanged a few more pleasantries and left the cool air-conditioned office.

The sun blazed down. Jessica and Karen were blinded by the strong light. They were surprised to see Pat outside.

"I knew you would be here. You should have called me and I would have brought you here."

"That's okay, Pat," said Jessica, "I wanted to meet the principal alone but Karen insisted on coming along."

"Any ideas on someone else we can see, Pat? Contacts near the school, or any restaurants nearby that young people visit?" asked Karen.

"A hospital, that's where we will go."

"Why?" asked Karen, "Jess would have been contacted if she was in one."

"Not necessarily," said Pat. "There have been cases where young Americans don't want their parents involved. Abortions, you know. Also, Carol may not have had her identity papers with her if she was injured. Her papers may have been taken from her at the time of the attempted kidnapping." He opened his car door for the ladies. Jessica in the back and Karen in the front seat.

Pat nudged close to rickshaws and other cars, turning onto side streets where hawkers were peddling their wares on the road. He waved them off when they offered to sell his guests plantains and guavas. They pulled up to a large two-storey white building. It did not look like a hospital from the outside. More like an embassy. It was guarded by a stony-faced security person who opened the large iron gate to let them in after Pat showed him his ID.

The reception area was well appointed. Fresh flowers were centred on the glass tables with cups and steaming teapots ready for visitors. This did not seem to be a public hospital where Jessica and Karen would have expected to find a more spartan environment.

Pat moved on ahead and spoke softly to the receptionist in Thai. He nodded to them and they approached the desk.

"You are Mrs. Guthrie?"

"Yes," said Jessica.

"If you are related to one of our previous patients and need some information, I would need to see your passport and driver's licence please."

Jessica opened her purse. "Darn. I left my papers at the hotel."

The receptionist smiled and said nothing.

"I have my passport," said Karen.

"Are you a relative?"

"No, but a very close friend."

"I'm sorry. We can only release information to close relatives who prove their identity."

Pat tried to intervene.

"Will any other ID be suitable?"

"If it is government issued."

"Oh, I have my Alberta Health Care Card. Here it is."

"This does not have your photograph, Mrs. Guthrie."

"I have a credit card."

"Sorry, Mrs. Guthrie. I need photo ID."

Pat looked up as someone entered the foyer.

"Pat! How nice to see you."

"Joseph! What a surprise! When did you start working here?"

"Last week. Do you need a new organ? I've got the right one for you, you devil."

The receptionist hesitated.

"Doctor. Do you know all these people?"

"I know Pat but I have not had the pleasure of meeting these charming ladies."

"These are my new friends visiting from Canada. Mrs. Guthrie and Mrs. Delaney."

"A pleasure. Are you here to see a patient?"

"No doctor, but they need information on a possible patient but don't have any picture ID," said the receptionist.

"Oh, forget the picture ID. Any friends of Pat can be trusted. Right Pat?" he winked.

"Dr. Joseph. My daughter Carol Guthrie may have been a patient here in the last few weeks."

"Aneka, please check the records for the last month."

Aneka checked. "I don't show any Carol Guthrie."

Jessica was not satisfied. "Do you show a patient who may have been Canadian with a similar sounding name? It may have been written down differently."

Aneka looked at Dr. Joseph for permission.

"Yes, please help our visitors."

The receptionist scrolled through the patients' records. "Sorry, no other similar sounding names and no Canadians."

"Thank you very much, Joseph. Pat, can we now go to the police station?"

"Sorry we can't help. What is this all about?" asked Joseph.

"It's a long story. Will tell you when I see you again. Have to rush now since we have a lot of places to visit," Pat ushered the ladies to the exit.

Chapter 17

"Pardon? That can't be...," said Len.

"I'm sorry, sir," the ticket agent said. "Your booking went through this morning but the credit card company has not authorized the transaction."

"Those sons of bitches!"

The agent returned his card. *The man was getting irate and seemed extremely nervous. She may have to call security.* Her finger was poised over the red button beneath the counter.

"I'm so sorry, miss, please excuse my language. I have had a bad week."

"Is there another credit card you have, sir?"

"Oh yes, of course. My MasterCard." He had forgotten that he had maxed out on his Visa card. What a difference in his life after Ben passed away. Money had never been a problem for Len when he worked for Ben.

"Let's run it through."

Len handed her the card and his passport. "It should be good for five thousand dollars, more than enough to cover the trip to Bangkok."

"It worked, Mr. Green. Let me print your ticket now."

Len was relieved. This trip could not be postponed.

"How many pieces of baggage?"

"Just my carry-on. This is a business trip, not a holiday." She returned his passport and the ticket.

"Thank you, miss." He ambled off towards the gate.

The Security agent looked at his boarding pass. Another person studied the X-ray of his bag.

"Please open your bag, sir."

Len unlocked it and the agent rummaged through the clothing.

"What is this, sir?"

"Oh, I forgot to take it out."

"You are not supposed to bring any liquids over one hundred millilitres on board the airplane, especially alcohol. The crew can deny you entry on the plane."

"I'm sorry."

"I need to confiscate the bottle."

"That's okay. Sorry."

Len headed towards the gate. *He should not have put whiskey in his bag. There would be enough on the plane.*

He arrived at the Vancouver airport. The gate for the connecting flight was not too far away and he hurried over.

The stewardess looked at Len shuffling down towards the entrance of the plane, and whispered to her colleague. "This one looks like trouble. Another alcoholic." She smiled at him and looked at his boarding pass.

"Towards the rear and to the left, sir."

The plane was half-full. Len was pleased that he may be able to get some sleep during this long trip. He had travelled often when he worked for Guthrie Construction but it had mostly been in First Class. He now had to adjust to flying Economy where they may restrict the number of drinks. Len had been drinking a lot since he left Guthrie Construction. His only close friend had been Ben. They would often go out to dinner and have a few drinks after a long day at work. He only realized how much he depended and cared for Ben after he was no longer there.

The plane picked up speed on the runaway and was soon airborne. The city soon disappeared below the clouds.

"I see you are an engineer," a passenger across the aisle extended his hand, which also had the iron ring on the little finger of the working hand which Canadian engineers wore.

"Yes, I used to work in Construction."

"Oh? One of the large multinationals?"

"No, a smaller company, Guthrie Construction."

"I'm a mechanical engineer with a Cooling Tower Manufacturer. We have a job in Bangkok."

"I have some opportunities in Bangkok I am pursuing too. Where did you go to school?"

"I graduated from Waterloo."

"Good university. I hired a few good engineers from there when I was working in Toronto."

"Why did you leave Guthrie Construction? Was it lack of work?"

"No. The owner, my boss, passed away suddenly. Unfortunately, the company was sold after that. A lot of us were very unhappy with the new owners who put profit ahead of quality. A lot of us left, or were pushed out."

"Disappointing, I am sure. My name is Carl and yours?"

"Len, Len Green."

"I've been quite lucky with my employment and have spent the last ten years with my company. The treat us very well."

Len sucked on the remnants of his whiskey and grunted. He didn't want to tell the young man what might lie ahead for him. Years and years with one company, giving it your everything and suddenly everything changed overnight. You thought you were so great and all of a sudden you were out on the street, pounding the pavement for a low-paying job during a recession. Watching your savings being drawn down, the temporary lift you get when you think an interview went well and later get a 'Dear John' letter. Finally taking a job outside your field and working for assholes who don't value your engineering education, or any education for that matter.

"Life is a bitch!"

"Pardon?"

"Sorry, I was talking to myself. Job prospects in Calgary are not good for most people in their fifties."

"Well, Len. I hope your opportunity in Bangkok works out well."

"I hope so too. Anything is better than Calgary at this time. All major projects are in limbo."

Len searched the seat pocket for headphones so that he could lose himself in a mindless movie. There were two to choose from "You Only Live Twice" and "Kidnapped."

He picked "Kidnapped", gestured the stewardess for another drink, put on the headphones and reclined his seat.

Chapter 18

Anu's captor held onto his hand firmly. So firmly it hurt.

"Don't do anything stupid," he hissed.

He tried to make eye contact with a couple who walked by, but they did not look at him. Instead, they were talking to each other, completely unaware of the danger that he was in despite his desperate gaze at them and his silent scream for help. A tuk-tuk came by with another passenger and stopped. Anu and his kidnapper got in. There was no escape now. They wedged him tightly between them and blocked the side view to any passing pedestrians.

"Remember, your mother is in good company now. Don't worry." The sarcastic tone was not missed by Anu. His poor mother being held by the other kidnapper and helpless at this time. Neither she, or Anu, could do anything for fear of harm coming to the other.

The tuk-tuk was now leaving Bangkok and moving into the countryside.

"I have a cap for you. Wear it now!" The kidnapper pulled out a black cap from his pocket and shoved it firmly on Anu's head. The man made sure the brim was covering his eyes so that he could not see where he was going. He pushed him backwards to seem like Anu was dozing in his seat to any curious passersby. The only sounds were that of the tuk-tuk, some buffalo in the distance, birds and monkeys in the trees. Anu was not familiar with the area outside of Bangkok since his mother had never taken him out of the city. After what seemed like an hour, the tuk-tuk turned, travelled onto a bumpy road going uphill and after a few minutes they stopped.

The kidnapper pushed down on his head so that he could not see. Both men held his arms firmly and pulled him into a doorway. He could hear the windows being closed and shuttered. They took off his cap and all he could see was a small oil lamp which provided a dim light for his prison. There was a small cot, a coffee table with a jug of water and some bowls on it. He smelled cooked rice and saw a couple of bananas and guavas on the table.

"You stay in this room and do not leave. The door will be locked from the outside. If you need anything, bang these pots together. But only if you need anything. Remember we are nearby and are keeping watch on you."

The two kidnappers left and locked the door from the outside. Anu heard them talk to the tuk-tuk driver and soon it left. He heard footsteps outside. It appeared that one of them had stayed behind to keep an eye on him.

He looked over his prison. It was one room with a small adjoining toilet. The two windows were closed and shuttered. He would try to look outside in a few moments when he was sure the man had moved farther away. He peered through the blinds and saw that this room was part of a larger apartment building. There was a courtyard with chickens and goats running loose. Two men were walking through the entrance to the courtyard. One of them looked like the man who had visited the shop. They sat down on a bench close to the entrance and lit their cigarettes, occasionally looking in the direction of his room and scanning the other areas of the yard. Anu suspected that they brought him here because one of them had likely seen him watch Miss Carol turn the corner with one of their conspirators.

He heard a chair being dragged across the floor in the room upstairs. The guards also looked up. There must be another prisoner upstairs he thought. He stood on the cot and tried to tap the ceiling but it was too high for him. Anu did not want to attract the attention of the guards so he sat on the cot to think what he could do next. The door did not look very sturdy. It was made of planks of wood nailed to an upper and lower plank. It would not be difficult to escape from this flimsy door if he had the right tools. It would be noisy though. An escape through the window was not possible because of bars to keep intruders out. There was a window in the toilet but it was too small to squeeze through. He would wait to see what the routine would be with the guards. They would likely open the door now and then to bring him food or to check on him. That may be the best time to escape. But where to? He was not sure where he was and what was outside the courtyard. There was no traffic noise so he assumed he was far from the road. He would have to be patient.

There were footsteps in the upper room and a door was opened and closed. Who could this person be?

Just then the two guards came towards his room. He quickly sat on his cot, expecting them to come in but they didn't. Instead, they just passed by, joking to each other. One remark he heard made his heart race. "Did you take care of the American girl today?" The other guard laughed and said something unintelligible. Anu was sure he now had company. Good company. He couldn't have wished for anything better. He must act soon and free Miss Carol. She must be in the room above.

Chapter 19

"There's no need to go to the police station," said Pat. "I already have a contact there who I have spoken to. He will meet us whenever you want."

"Great! Can we meet him today?" asked Jessica.

"Sure, I can try to set something up for this afternoon. Are you OK with that?"

"The sooner the better."

Pat checked his contacts on his cellphone, found what he needed and dialed. He spoke in Thai, nodded and smiled.

"Two o'clock is fine. We have a meeting place arranged."

"You are so well-organized Pat!" Karen squeezed his arm.

"I'll pick you up at one-thirty at the hotel." Pat shook Jessica's hand, gave Karen a hug and left.

"He's such a big help," gushed Karen.

"I hope his contact will provide us with some useful information. Wherever Carol is, we need to get to her as soon as possible. The more time lost will make it more difficult to track her down. I miss her so much. How could this have happened so suddenly? She seemed to be so happy here."

"Don't worry, Jess. Pat seems to have all the right contacts. Kidnapping must happen here quite often. Len sure gave us the right person to work with. Maybe Suttikul was right and Carol might have gone on a secret rendezvous with a boy-friend who is as charming as Pat."

They parted and went to their rooms. Jessica was beginning to have a good feeling that she would see Carol in the next few days. Len had really been kind to engage Pat in this search. Karen was right. He appeared to be the right person for the job. She wondered about his other job and if the absence from his work may cause a problem. She would ask him and offer something to make up for his lost wages. She wondered about Jariya. *Should she try to make contact with Jariya by herself, or should she ask Pat to come along?* She was leaning to the former since she did not want to impose on Pat too much. She might try to contact the school again tomorrow to see if the student had returned. He may provide some good clues if he was the last person to see Carol.

As she was opened her door, she heard a sound in her room. Her heart pounded and she slammed the door shut. A chambermaid in the corridor looked up and asked, "Anything wrong, miss? Please, can I help?"

"It's alright, thank you. I was only startled by a noise in my room."

"What you fear?" the chambermaid persisted.

"I just heard someone or something in my room."

"You stay here and I will check."

Jessica did not say anything but let the maid go in. She came out a moment later.

"Look okay in room, nobody there. Sometimes monkeys bang on window."

"Oh, maybe that is what it was. Thank you."

Jessica smiled at the chambermaid and entered her room. Everything was in order. She would check on Karen and knocked on the door. There was no answer. She knocked once more and then decided to wait in case Karen was in the toilet. She caught the attention of the chambermaid again.

"Just checking to see if my friend is in her room."

"Oh, lady left room little while ago."

"Oh, thank you."

Jessica went down to the lobby to search for her but she was not there. She checked the souvenir shop, took a quick look in the restaurant but there was no sign of her friend. *She would not have left the hotel without telling me* thought Jessica.

"Mrs. Guthrie," the concierge handed her a note.

Pat and I are just going for a spin. Be back soon. Love, Karen.

She could have knocked on my door, Jessica thought as she went back to her room. She removed her cellphone from her pocket. Perhaps there were unread text messages from Karen.

New Message was flashing on the screen. She pressed *View Message.*

"See you soon. K."

Jessica went back to her room and lay on the bed to have a little nap. She would need it.

Chapter 20

The Thai Customs agent made eye contact with the overweight foreigner. He was sweating and appeared very uncomfortable. He may be a sex tourist. Len fumbled in his coat pocket for his passport.

"Why you come to Thailand?"

"Oh, I have some business here."

"What type of business?"

"I am an engineer."

The agent hesitated. Engineers from Canada, the US and Britain often visited Bangkok on business but most of them were seldom nervous when he interviewed them. This was an odd fellow. Perhaps he should detain him.

"Which company you work for?"

"A Canadian company. Guthrie Construction."

"What business they have in Thailand?"

"We don't have any projects in Thailand. That is why I am here. I am looking for business opportunities. My company does lots of work in Canada and the United States."

Len steadied himself. He must appear more relaxed to stop further questions.

"You have business card?"

Len opened his wallet and handed a Guthrie Construction business card to the agent. He was never able to discard the cards since they had such fond memories for him.

"You Chief Engineer for Guthrie Construction?" The agent was impressed that this man had such a high position in his company.

"Yes."

"Welcome to Thailand, Mr. Green! Hope you find good work in Bangkok. Maybe provide some jobs for my countrymen?"

Len hid his relief, ambled towards the exit and hailed a taxi.

"Which hotel, sir?"

"There is one close to *The Hilton*. I forget its name."

"Oh, couple of hotels there, sir, but I will drive you. One is *Plaza Hotel* and other is *The Majestic*."

"Ah, I remember now. It is *The Majestic*."

"OK, sir. We will be there in thirty minutes. Lots of traffic since it is holiday in Thailand today."

"Which holiday is it?"

"Coronation Day, sir. His Majesty King Bhumibol and his ancestors are honoured today.

He very good king. People like him but not the government."

Len was tired but did want to know more about Thailand. The taxi driver was a pleasant fellow.

"What's wrong with the government?"

"Too much corruption and crime on streets is getting bad. Too many poor people and not enough work. Not like old days when everyone happy and everyone have job. You stay in Bangkok or go outside?"

"I have business in Bangkok."

"Oh good! What business, sir?"

"Engineering."

"Oh, that is good business. Bangkok need new roads and bridges. Government spend no money on repair. Only paint, no fix. Man fell through old bridge and died in river last month."

Len's interest was aroused. He wished he was back with Guthrie in that job he loved so much. That was his life. Here he was in a land that needed people like him but his business with Jessica was more important. He hoped she had warmed up to Pat. Len had not told Jessica he would be visiting and had asked Pat not to tell her either.

It would be a surprise. Kind of...

Chapter 21

Voices of the guards came closer to his prison. Anu tensed as the door was unlocked. Only one guard was in the doorway with a tin plate with some rice and a banana. A mug of lukewarm tea was also handed to him. The guard grunted and locked the door again. He heard the other guard's footfalls upstairs but could not hear any voices from the room above. When he could hear no more sounds he peeked through the crack in the door. The two men sat at the entrance to the courtyard smoking and drinking tea. He peered out at the courtyard again to see of there were any other persons there besides the two. The crack did not give him a proper view of the compound and he was not sure these were the only people present. The guards did not appear to live in any rooms in this building. They continued to sit at the entrance smoking and chatting. It was possible that only the guards, the prisoner upstairs and Anu, were in this compound.

He could hear a tuk-tuk approach. He looked out of the crack again and saw two men getting out. The guards rose to meet them but the two newcomers started shouting at them and pushed them aside. The guards continued to stay at the entrance while the two men came towards the house. He sat on his cot in fear, assuming they were going to hurt him or take him away to another place. He heard them run upstairs. A few moments later the upstairs door slammed shut. Through the crack he could see the two men as they were leaving. Between them, he was certain, was Miss Carol, with her hands tied behind her back and a hat pulled down over her eyes. The men shouted something at the guards, pulled Carol into the tuk-tuk and sped off.

The guards came towards his room. He sat on the cot preparing for the worst. The door was opened.

"You can go now."

"What?"

"You can leave, go now, soon!"

Anu did not wait to ask any more questions but quickly left the room and ran out of the courtyard, in case they changed their minds. He could see the tuk-tuk in the distance in a cloud of dust and began to run down the dirt road which he hoped would lead to the city. There were no buildings or houses that he could see near the road. He hoped he could get to the city before nightfall.

The isolated countryside likely had predators, animals or humans. He feared the latter more.

Chapter 22

Jessica awoke in the darkness. She had only wanted to nap, instead she had fallen into a deep sleep. The clock in the room showed it was almost ten thirty at night. Why hadn't Karen come to her room? Perhaps she did but she had not heard her knocking since she had been in dreamland, or nightmare land. She opened the door and went to Karen's room and tapped gently on the door. No answer.

"Karen! Are you in there?"

No sound. Perhaps she was still with Pat. Her cellphone did not show any text messages or missed calls. She called Karen but there was no answer. She sent a text message to ask where she was. Maybe they were in the restaurant downstairs. She took the elevator to the main floor.

"Would you like to have dinner, madam?"

"I want to see if my friends are here."

"Certainly, please walk in and look around."

In the dimly-lit dining room, there were a few couples at the tables. Pat and Karen were not among them.

"Hope to see you later, madam."

At reception she asked if Karen had returned, or left a message for her.

"Would you like to call her room?"

"I already knocked at the door but there was no answer. Can you please ring her?"

The desk clerk obliged and dialed the room. He smiled as he waited for the phone to be picked up. After a number of rings, he shook his head.

"Does not seem to be in room. Perhaps she still out with her friend."

This bothered Jessica since she knew that Karen would have sent her a text message or left a note to say she would be late, even though she was out with Pat. This was not good.

She sat down in the reception area with her cellphone. 'Where are you?' she texted again. An hour passed and she went back to the restaurant and ordered a glass of wine and a salad. Things were not working out. Why had Karen not come back earlier? Why had she not left a message?

It was too late to go outside for some fresh air so she went up to her room and switched on the television. She was pleased to see that most of the stations the hotel had selected broadcasted in English.

Last night two female tourists were reported missing by their travelling companions. One girl, eighteen years old, an Australian, was here on a hiking trip with her friends. The other, an American, was on her way to Phuket. Both had last been seen at a popular bar on Mysore street in Bangkok. Police report that there is no reason to panic since it is not uncommon for young girls to visit other friends in Bangkok without informing their travelling companions. They will continue to monitor the situation.

Jessica switched off the set. This was not the type of news she wished to listen to. More girls who disappeared added to her fear that there must be an organized crime ring in the city that preyed on young western women.

She could not sleep. The traffic and noise outside seemed louder now. She checked her cellphone but there was no recent activity. *Karen may be in danger too. What a mess!* She turned off the light and lay in the bed, knowing she would not sleep but expected to focus more in the dark. She heard voices in the corridor and footsteps walking by her room. If it was Karen, she would have knocked.

More footsteps. Someone had stopped outside in the hallway outside her door. She heard the rustle of paper being pushed under the door. She quickly put the light on and saw an envelope on the carpet. Rather than opening it, she opened the door and looked down the corridor. No one could be seen. Whoever it was had moved quite fast. She ripped open the envelope. A note was enclosed.

'If you want see your daughter will cost US one million. Transfer details will be given you. Have funds ready for transfer in five days. Wait further instructions. Calling police not good idea. Daughter may suffer.'

Chapter 23

Karen felt very comfortable with Pat as they motored through Bangkok's trendy district. Skyscrapers, boutiques and the absence of large crowds was a pleasant treat for her. "There must be quite a few rich people in Bangkok."

"A few. This is a rich city. It is the countryside which suffers because of the city. All the work is here in the city. Banking, tourism, restaurants, theatres and so on. Outside are peasants who work in fields for rich landlords. Tourism is good in Thailand but there is a bad side as I mentioned before."

"You had told us about the sex trade and we immediately thought Carol has been kidnapped for this purpose."

"Maybe, but not likely. Organized crime brings in sex trade workers from the Philippines, India and China, but white women are brought in mainly from the former Soviet Union republics. These young girls are led to believe that they can get jobs as maids or waitresses in good restaurants but end up in brothels working for dangerous criminals."

"So where might Carol be?"

"There are some kidnappings for ransom. My police officer contact has confirmed there have been a few cases in the last year. With the Internet, it is possible to check on local tourists, especially young people, and find out whether their families are rich or poor. The kidnappers have contacts in the local bars. These people chat with new customers, find out where they are from, ask if their parents are with them, and get lots of information from naïve young people. It is likely that Carol is a kidnapping victim for this purpose."

Pat pulled the car into a parking lot near the waterfront. Several small boats were anchored close to the beach. Farther out to sea, lights twinkled on the luxurious passenger ships. Rich tourists with lots of money likely sampled caviar and sipped champagne on board, while the poor of Thailand struggled in their shitholes, scavenging food just like the rats around their huts.

"Let's have a little walk here, if you are not too tired," said Pat.

"Good idea. I need a little bit of exercise." Karen linked her arm in Pat's.

"Will we see you in Calgary one day?"

"Maybe," said Pat. "Depends on the work situation. At this time, I have enough work here but who knows how long it will continue."

A ship's horn sounded in the distance, just as Karen's phone beeped with an incoming text message, which she didn't hear. They continued farther. Pat seemed lost in thought and did not venture further talk. Karen was starting to tire and suggested they return to the hotel.

Behind them there were quick, heavy footsteps. They turned just as two men jumped out of the shadows and grabbed Karen. Pat pulled her away but the two kicked him and shoved him to the ground and started to punch him. One pulled a gun and said something in Thai. Pat turned to Karen, "Run now! Fast!"

"But..." she stuttered.

"No, run. Go away from here! They want you, not me."

Karen turned and ran past the car onto a street. She heard a gunshot behind her. She waved her hands to passing motorists but they only honked and waved back. She gave up on trying to stop the passing cars and ran into a nearby shop.

"Please help."

The old shopkeeper shook his head and said something in Thai. She assumed he did not understand her. She ran into another larger store.

"Please, my friend has been shot and is being held by two men."

The young store worker took her to the Manager and said something in Thai.

"What is it, Miss?"

"My friend has been attacked and is not far away. Can you help us?"

"I phone police now." He grabbed a phone and dialled, nodded to Karen, spoke quickly in Thai and put the phone down.

"Police will be here in few minutes, don't worry. Don't go out. Too dangerous."

Karen agreed that there was no point in her going back because she couldn't do anything. After what seemed like half an hour a police car arrived. Two officers got out of the car and came into the shop. The manager called to them and pointed to Karen.

"What is problem, Miss?"

Karen explained what happened. They asked her to get in the car and drive with them to the scene. Pat's car was gone. There was no sign of Pat or the two men.

"Where it happen?"

"Here," she said and pointed to the spot where she had just left. The officers took out their flashlights to light the pathway.

"You sure your friend shot? Cannot see signs of blood on ground."

They walked farther down the path and looked in the nearby bushes. After spending fifteen minutes or so they stopped.

"Miss, you come with us to station to make statement."

She agreed and they drove through the busy streets. Karen kept scanning all the cars to see if one of them was Pat's, but did not see a Mustang.

The police station was small. A short, fat officer was at the desk. The two officers spoke to him for a few minutes and then left.

"Please sit," the man said. He seemed quite bored.

"Here is pen and paper. Please write your name, and hotel. Also write what happened."

Karen did not see any point in talking to the officer. She nodded, took the pen and started to write. The man opened a brown paper bag and started to eat some aromatic dumplings. He sucked on a mug of tea and looked at her as she wrote. She put the pen down.

"Investigation process is three hundred baht."

"Pardon?"

"You pay me three hundred baht for police to do work."

"Why?"

"We need to buy paper, pens, gasoline for police cars, telephone. This is way police work in Thailand."

This was a surprise for Karen. "Will you give me a receipt?"

"I give you receipt when you give me money."

She did not have her purse with her and had elected not to bring it along since they didn't intend to go shopping. All she had was her cellphone and she did not want to call Jessica and add further to her troubles.

"My money is at the hotel."

"Then I keep statement and start work when you bring money from hotel."

The officer ate another dumpling and sucked more tea from his mug. "Ok, Miss, see you later. Sorry for your bad experience in Bangkok."

Karen left the station and called a passing tuk-tuk since she did not see any taxis on the street. The driver stopped and she got in. "*The Metropole Hotel* please."

The driver nodded and weaved into the traffic at high speed. She held onto the armrests in the tuk-tuk while the driver veered into any available break in the traffic. At the hotel she asked him to wait and she would bring him the fare of ten baht. She went to the desk and asked the receptionist for the money and asked him to put it on the bill. The driver thanked her and drove away.

She took the elevator and ran down the corridor to Jessica's room and banged on the door. There was no answer.

"Shit!"

Karen entered her room. Her luggage had been opened and her clothes were all over the bed. She looked around to see if anyone was in the bathroom. It was obvious whoever was there had been in a great hurry. Her passport and money were still there. There did not seem to be anything missing. She called Reception.

"Has someone been in my room this evening?"

"Your friend, Mrs. Guthrie, was looking for you. Maybe she was in your room."

"No, someone has been in my room and opened my suitcase."

"I send someone up right away, Miss."

A few moments later there was a gentle tap on her door. She opened it. It was a uniformed hotel security guard. He looked around the room and checked the window to ensure it was still closed. He examined the area around the door latch to see if someone had forced it open.

"Anything missing, Miss?"

"No."

"I will make report to Manager. So sorry, Miss. This is good hotel. All staff are good people. Someone from outside must have come in. If items missing, please let me know and I will contact police."

"Thank you, that will be all."

The guard left and Karen sat on the bed. What could she do? She must find Jessica first. What about Pat? She must go back to the police station with the hope that they had found him.

Chapter 24

It would be a long walk to the city along this dirt road. It did not seem to be well used and the forest would be alive soon with predators. Anu had grown up in the city and had never been in the jungle before. If someone was with him it may have been a good experience. Mosquitoes buzzed around him. Lots of mosquitoes, much more than in the city. He swatted as many as he could but they enveloped him in a cloud. He waved his hands to drive them off and hoped that he could get to the city sooner.

A car was approaching from behind. He turned. It was a small black car with only the driver in it. He heard the engine slowing and was not sure whether he should be happy or scared. The car pulled alongside him. A westerner was driving it.

"Hello, young man. Do you need a ride?" He was an American or a Canadian. The car was quite new, probably a rental.

"Yes, please," he said and opened the door to get in. Immediately he smelled alcohol in the car.

The man smiled and asked, "Where do you live, young man?"

"In Bangkok, sir."

"Oh, don't 'sir' me please, call me Walter. I'm from New York on a holiday in your beautiful country." He patted Anu on his head.

"Your wife not come along?"

"No, I'm not married. Don't want to be tied down, you know. I like being single."

Anu was suspicious. His knowledge of older westerners travelling alone meant two things: they were either academics or sexual predators. He was inclined to believe the latter since academics usually travelled in groups, or with another companion.

"Are you hungry?"

"Yes," Anu said.

"OK. We can stop in the city for a bite. Does that suit you?"

"Yes, sir."

"Walter, or if you wish you can call me 'Uncle Walter'. Children in my neighbourhood call me Uncle Walter you know. Lots of them around. They love to visit me. I always have lots of candy for them. Do you like candy?"

"Yes."

Walter pulled out a chocolate bar and gave it to Anu who politely began to eat it.

"I know nice restaurant where we go."

"OK, you direct me when we get into the city."

Anu had a plan and he wanted to get closer to his neighbourhood first.

"Bangkok is big city. Many nice young girls."

"I'm not much of a lady's man. I've always been shy with girls. My mother was always trying to fix me up. Ha, ha!"

Anu decided to change the subject. It was clear Walter had no interest in women. His interest seemed to be with boys, young boys.

"New York, very big city?"

"Oh yes, it is huge. I live outside New York. Away from the busy places. I teach in a school there."

"You look like teacher."

"How can you tell?"

"You look like clever man. My teachers very clever." Anu continued to be friendly and appear naïve to Walter. His eyes searched the roadside for a possible quick escape.

Baiyoke Tower was now visible as they moved closer to the city. It was getting dark and they should arrive in the city within the next thirty minutes or so. Huts and street vendors now lined the roadway. He was preparing for his next move.

"Would you like to see a movie after we get something to eat?" asked Walter as he rested his hand on Anu's lap. Anu did not flinch and pretended to expect that gesture. He smiled back at Walter.

"Yes, Uncle Walter. First, we must go to my favourite restaurant. Not far from here."

Walter grinned as Anu gave him directions to the restaurant. They came to a stop light.

"What are you doing?" asked Walter, as Anu opened the door and darted out onto the crowded street, relieved that escape was so easy. He ran as far as he could, in case he was still visible to Walter, and then started to walk. His home was not far away now and he let out his breath in relief. He opened the door and called out to his mother. The house was empty. He ran to their shop. Thankfully his mother was there.

"Anu! My dear Anu. Are you hurt?" She hugged him.

"No, Mama. Did they hurt you?"

"No, they left soon after you had gone. I thought I would not see you again."

"They still have Miss Carol. That was who they wanted. I must find her."

"You can't do it alone, you need help."

"I don't trust the police."

"Neither do I, but who else is there?"

"Maybe my school principal. I will see him in school tomorrow and ask how he can help."

"Come, let us go home now. You need to eat some food and tell me what happened."

They walked home and Anu was not as worried as he was before. He knew now that they were not interested in him anymore. *Miss Carol was in danger. She had been so close. Why could he not have done something while they were both prisoners in the same building? He should have tried harder to escape from the room and rescue her.*

Chapter 25

"Your passport, sir."

"I have a reservation."

"We know, Mr. Green. But hotel need picture ID."

Len gave the desk clerk his passport. He looked at it nodded, and gave it back.

"Would you like non-smoking room, sir? Your booking not tell type of room."

"Non-smoking, please. I would however prefer a room no higher than the fifth floor."

"Certainly, sir. Here is one. Room 420."

The clerk passed him the room key and Len moved towards the elevator. Another couple was waiting.

"Good afternoon," said Len.

"Hello. Is this your first day in Bangkok?" asked the man.

"Yes. I have a lot to find out."

The elevator doors opened and they entered. Len stayed silent. He was too tired to engage in small talk.

"I see you are from Canada," said the woman.

"Oh, very observant. My Air Canada luggage tag is still on."

"I have a sister in Canada. In Toronto."

"I used to live in Toronto. Great city," said Len as the elevator stopped at the fifth floor. "Nice meeting you."

"Enjoy your stay in Bangkok."

"I will, thank you."

Len opened the drapes and looked out onto the street below. Tuk-tuks, taxis, rickshaws and many cyclists filled the street below. Very different from downtown Calgary where, as he was often told by his friends in Toronto, they rolled up the sidewalks after nine o'clock in the evening. He opened his suitcase and took out his notebook. He found Jessica's hotel phone number and rechecked Pat's cellphone number. He should call Pat first.

"Operator, please put me through to 02-444-9966."

"Please hold, Mr. Green, while I dial number." The operator connected him but there was no answer, so he hung up.

Must have taken a fancy to the two women. Probably entertaining them in a fine restaurant he thought. He lay down on the bed. It had been a very tiring and stressful journey and sleep came quickly.

He awoke with a start. It was dark outside and he thought he had heard gunshots. Outside the window he saw a tuk-tuk moving away, backfiring as it drove off. It was three in the morning. He wondered if he could get something to eat at this hour and went down to the lobby. The desk clerk told him the restaurant was closed, but down the street he may find some small cafes or bars which were open all night. The humidity was oppressive as he ambled down the street. It was not as busy but there were more people out now that there were in downtown Calgary in the evening. Neon lights cast red, green and blue light on the street vendors offering coconut water, bananas and papayas along the busy roadways.

"Looking for girl friend?"

Len turned around. A young boy smiled and pulled out some pictures of young girls in hot pants and bikinis. Len shook his head but the boy persisted.

"Young girls, fifteen. Lots of experience with men. You will have good time."

"No thank you."

"Only fifty baht for thirty minutes. Can do massage too."

Len hurried along and ignored the boy. Out of the shadows appeared two young girls.

"Hello, Mister! You want to have good time tonight?"

The boy behind him yelled to them in Thai and they yelled back.

How can this be allowed to happen? Young boys and girls involved in the sex trade. What a disgrace. Probably it was Westerners who corrupted this country.

He was not sleepy yet and did not want to go back to the hotel. Instead, he felt he could escape the soliciting on the street by going into a nearby bar which he entered. Cigarette smoke thickened the atmosphere of this dimly lit bar called *The Damsels Den*. A scantily clad girl on a small stage danced seductively while other tourists and locals sipped their drinks and conversed. He had not frequented these types of bars since he was a student in university. He hadn't liked it then and his impression had not changed. He sat down at an empty table.

"Something to drink sir?"

The waitress took his order for a beer and returned quickly with it. "Anything else, sir?"

"No, thank you."

He sipped his beer and wished Pat was with him. He was not comfortable alone in a bar in a foreign country. He felt a hand on his shoulder and turned around.

"May I join you?"

It was an attractive young girl. A local. He hesitated, but she sat down anyway and looked intently at him.

"Where you from?"

"Canada."

"Oh, I have met many Canadians here. Bangkok good place for Canadian tourists."

"You work here?"

"I work in office. In evening I do part time work."

"What work is that?"

"I dance with customers. Would you like to dance with me?"

"I don't dance, thank you."

"You buy me drink, maybe?"

Len did not know how to get rid of her but needed the company.

"Yes, and order another beer for me."

She called the waitress and ordered something, speaking only Thai. The waitress smiled, nodded and went away, bringing her back what was probably a Bloody Mary.

"My name Daisy. What your name?"

"Len."

"First time in Bangkok?"

"First time in Thailand, yes."

He never thought that he would be making small talk with a young woman, especially this type of woman, likely a Lady of the Night. His eyes moved to the stage where the dancer was taking off her top. He then looked at the young woman's cleavage.

Why am I behaving this way? I must pull myself together he thought.

Daisy reached over and stroked his hand. "You look worried, very worried. Your business not doing well?"

"I'm fine. I am here to help a friend. She is in trouble."

"Oh, she Thai girl? Maybe into drugs, having problem with pimp?"

"No, no, nothing like that. She was the wife of my old boss."

"You friends with your boss's wife? Oo la la. Must be nice."

"It's not what you think. He passed away in Canada some years ago. His wife is her now, looking for her daughter."

"Daughter run away from home?" Daisy asked. "I left home too, when I was twelve. Father not good, he no work and he beat me and my mother. I ran away with boy friend."

Len gulped down his beer. "I must go now."

"You want massage maybe, help you sleep."

Len grunted, gave her twenty baht and left the bar. A tuk-tuk almost ran into him when he stepped onto the street. *He must get back to the hotel. He had seen enough of the seedy side of Thai nightlife.*

Chapter 26

Jessica returned to the hotel after spending some time walking around in the hotel garden to calm herself. She checked her cellphone again. No messages from Karen.

"Jessica!"

It was Karen. She had just got out of the elevator.

"Pat has been shot!"

"What?!"

Karen related the incident to her, including her bad experience at the police station. Jessica told her about the note slipped under her door.

"It's too late now to do anything. We will have to wait until morning."

"Also, someone was in my room. I'm scared, Jessica. I have not been so scared since I was a child at a scary movie."

"There is another bed in my room, maybe we should stay together tonight," suggested Jessica.

"I'd like that."

They talked more about the evening's happenings and watched TV until Karen settled down. Jet lag was setting in again and it wasn't long before they both fell asleep. A loud knock at the door awoke Jessica. The clock showed it was past noon.

"Just a minute," she called out. She peered through the peephole. It was a hotel worker. She opened the door slightly, and kept the chain-lock on.

"Mrs. Guthrie? Man waiting in reception for you. Your phone off hook. Sorry."

"Please tell him to wait a few minutes. I will be down shortly."

Perhaps it was Pat. Maybe he is OK. She woke Karen.

"A man is downstairs. It may be Pat. I will go and check."

After a quick shower, Jessica went to the lobby.

"Jessica! Where's Karen?"

"Are you OK?" she asked.

"I'm fine, where's Karen?"

"She's in my room. She thought you had been killed."

"No, they just shot past me and roughed me up and gave me a message for you."

"For me?!"

"Yes. They have Carol."

Jessica was overjoyed for a moment and thought *She's alive, thank God!*

"Where is she?"

"All they told me is that you must not go to the police."

"I know, they left a note under my door."

"They have another message they want me to pass on to you. These men seem to be a part of an organized crime ring. They said she is safe but they want a million US dollars."

"Pat!"

It was Karen. She rushed to Pat and hugged him. He winced as she touched his hand.

"I thought you had been killed."

"Would take a lot more to kill me. I have lived in Bangkok long enough. These guys didn't want to kill me, they just needed to reinforce their message to Jessica."

Jessica turned to Karen. "They have Carol and want a ransom."

"She's alive and safe!" Karen hugged Jessica. Pat was not his usual bouncy self. He hadn't shaved and his eyes drooped like he had lost some sleep.

"I was trying to phone you and Karen but got no answer. They blindfolded me and took me in their car and dropped me off outside the city limits. I had to walk for an hour or so before I got in and caught a taxi and then got to my car. I left my phone in the car, cleverly."

"Pat, you can use a coffee."

They went to the hotel restaurant.

"I made a report at the police station, but was not taken seriously. They wanted money to process the case."

"That's normal. It's not a bribe," said Pat. "They need to cover their admin costs. Don't worry, I will call them tomorrow."

Jessica sipped her coffee. "What else did they say about Carol?"

"All they said was that she was in good hands. These are just hired thugs. Messengers. Who knows what their boss is like? Maybe a Russian or a Turk."

"How do I get one million US dollars in a few days?"

"I'll take you to a bank tomorrow and ask how a transfer can be arranged."

"I don't have a million sitting in an account, Pat!"

"That's what we can talk to the bank about. Maybe they will give you a loan."

"Why would a bank loan a tourist one million dollars?" asked Jessica.

"Do you have some friends who can wire you money?"

"Fat chance. I can come up with two-hundred-thousand in the next week, but not one million."

"I can loan you some money, Jess," offered Karen.

"Let's see when they make contact again. Maybe we can negotiate with them," Pat suggested.

Jessica did not like this. How could she raise so much money so quickly? Most of her money was tied up in real estate and some fixed investments and it would take at least a month, if not more, to get a million dollars in cash.

"I should leave you to rest for awhile. I'll see you later." Pat gave them both a hug and left.

Laughter and giggling continued around them. The waiter came by to ask if they needed more coffee or some food, but they declined.

"I will make a few calls from the hotel room to discuss my funds with my financial advisor."

"Why can't we use a cellphone?" asked Karen.

"Ah, you probably didn't know. Cellphone calls can be listened to by many hackers. It's best to use a landline when making confidential calls."

"How did you know that?" asked Karen.

"Learned it from Ben. He never used his cell for any major business calls. Always used the good old-fashioned, plug-in telephone. Besides, didn't you read about the Prince of Wales's private cellphone calls to Camilla?"

Jessica fished out a business card from her purse.

"Henry Higginbotham?! A Financial Advisor with a name like that? He would be more suitable as the Prince's cousin! Hopefully he treats you royally."

"It gets worse, his wife's name is Hilary Regina Higginbotham. She has HRH on her necklace."

Karen laughed while Jessica dialed the operator.

"A long-distance call to Canada please. The number is 403 288 5638."

"A moment please, Mrs. Guthrie."

"Long distance for Mr. Higginbotham please," said Jessica to the Royal Bank of Canada operator.

"He is with someone now. Can I take a message?"

"Can you please tell him it is Mrs. Guthrie. It is very urgent. This is long distance and I am calling from Bangkok, Thailand."

"Just a minute, please. I will check."

In a few moments Higginbotham was on the line.

"Jessica?"

"Yes, it's me."

"OK, shoot, what is the urgency and how can I help?"

"I need one million dollars US within five days."

"What?!"

"Carol has been kidnapped and that is the ransom."

There was a silence on the other end.

"Hello, are you still there?"

"Yes, I am Jessica. I was just a bit flabbergasted. I know Carol too. It is a big shock for me."

"Can you get the money to me here in Bangkok?"

"That is a lot of money to get together in five days. There will be lots of questions raised by my manager since large transfers like this to an individual in another country may require Bank of Canada approval. Procedures are tighter now due to money laundering. It's not going to be easy, Jessica. It may look like dirty money being exchanged. Five days will be difficult."

"What is the maximum you can transfer over within five days? Maybe we can negotiate with the kidnappers and buy some more time."

"Not sure, I will need to look into this deeper. The authorities here need to be informed regarding such a large transaction. That may take longer."

Jessica asked Higginbotham to call her back at the hotel. She gave him the hotel number and hung up.

Henry called back within fifteen minutes. "Jessica, I could transfer two hundred and fifty thousand within five days but am not sure that one million could be done within that time frame. It will be at least ten days. I will call again and tell you which Bangkok affiliated bank we would need to deal with for the transfer. The Canadian Embassy in Bangkok should be told about Carol being missing. They will start expediting the appropriate officials to get involved discreetly. Good luck. Keep the faith."

Jessica hung up. "A good start. Let's go to the bar and have a drink."

At times like this perhaps alcohol could help.

Chapter 27

"Anu, were you sick yesterday?" asked his teacher.

"Yes," he lied, not wanting to discuss his kidnapping experience of two days ago.

"The principal wanted to see you yesterday. You should go to see him now. It must be very important for him to call you to his office. Did you do something naughty the day before, to miss school yesterday?"

"No," he said. Maybe Miss Carol was back in the school, maybe they had let her go like they did with him. His joy was short-lived.

"Young man, why were you absent yesterday? Were you sick, and if so, do you have a letter from your mother?"

"No, sir." Mr. Suttikul could be very intimidating. Anu had seen him cane other students for minor misdemeanours. He started to steel himself, expecting a beating. He would not cry like the other boys. He watched Mr. Suttikul's gold watch. He dared not look at his stern face. Students did not make eye contact with their superiors, teachers included, principals most of all. They could beat, expel or prevent a student from entering other schools. This was a very desirable profession, especially for the power hungry and sadistic persons. Corporal punishment was an accepted way to deal with children. *If that didn't improve discipline what would?* the teachers thought.

"Miss Carol's mother visited me yesterday. You should have been here."

"Miss Carol's mother?" She had not mentioned that her mother was in Bangkok.

"She wanted to ask you about the last time you saw Miss Carol. She is still missing. Her mother is very worried and I want to help her. She seems to be a very important lady in Canada. Maybe a business woman or maybe a politician or a politician's wife."

"Sir. I was kidnapped on Monday, after school." Anu then told Mr. Suttikul all that had happened and his feeling that Carol was in the room above his at the temporary prison. Suttikul made copious notes and interrupted frequently to ask for clarification. Anu did not mention the man who had given him a ride after he had been released. This was not necessary. Furthermore, an event like this was not unusual in Bangkok and police did nothing to antagonize tourists, as his mother had found out.

"Do you know how to get to that place if I drove you in my car?"

"I cannot guide you, sir. My captors had pulled a cap over my eyes while driving me there in a tuk-tuk. After I was released and walked down the road a tourist brought me into the city. But Miss Carol is not there anymore. They took her to another place."

"Umm... I will contact her mother. Make sure you are in school tomorrow, young man. Be careful on the way home. Run fast if you see anyone suspicious but I don't think they are interested in you anymore."

"Yes, sir. Thank you."

Anu went back to the classroom. He felt much happier now that the principal was going to help too. There may not be much time. They may have taken Miss Carol to another place farther away from Bangkok. He could not concentrate during the lessons and was glad when the bell finally rang. He hurried home and told his mother that the principal would help. She was relieved. She did not want Anu trying anything alone. Taneka sensed that her son was experiencing 'puppy love'. She was afraid that his infatuation may lead him to try to make a heroic rescue.

Anu pulled out his school books from his bag to do his home work. Math, Physics, Chemistry.

It was a lot of work. *Can he get all this done tonight?* He had so much on his mind. He spread his books over the table while his mother put hot coals in the iron to press his school clothes for the morning. He started to read the assignment. It made no sense. He read it again. Miss Carol was in danger and here he was doing his homework. He sighed.

"Anu, don't worry, Miss Carol will be found. All they want is the money. If they wanted to harm her, they would have done so by now and we would have heard about it."

He nodded and continued to attempt to do his school work. Taneka ironed his school uniform, folded his socks and put them by his shoes. She noticed that he had fallen asleep on the table. She gently shook him awake and took him to his cot and kissed him good night.

She started to tidy up his books to put them in his school bag. She noticed a drawing. It was a girl. Long hair, large eyes, wearing long pants and a T-shirt, with a Canadian flag. She smiled. *Her little son was experiencing love. Another phase in his young life.* Taneka could not protect him like a man could in this country and she wished he had a real father. She was glad that the principal was stepping in to save Anu's damsel in distress.

Chapter 28

Pat was alone in his apartment. He checked his phone. Someone had called but had not left a message. Call Display showed the number but not the name. He called the number.

"Majestic Hotel."

Pat knew it must be Len. "Put me through to Len Green's room please."

"A moment, sir."

The phone rang, once, twice and continued. The operator did not intercept, so he called back.

"Mr. Len Green is not answering. Please let him know that Pattama Jainukul called."

He began to tidy up his apartment. He hoped that Karen would stay with him but felt that she would not leave Jessica alone. Maybe he could bring her here for a drink, by herself. She had warmed up to him and he quite liked her. If only his life was not such a mess. Her experience at the harbour must have terrified her and he wished that hadn't happened. His phone rang.

"Pat?"

"Len! How are you, my friend?"

"Good, but tired!"

"I'll bet. It was a long journey for you."

"Feels even longer when you get older." Len yawned.

"Do you want me to come over now?"

"Whenever you want to. If I'm napping, bang hard on the door. I'm in Room 420."

"I'm doing a few chores and should be there by six." He hung up.

Pat had known Len when he worked in Toronto. As Chief Engineer of Guthrie Construction, Len had asked him to set up their Computing Systems. They continued a business association for the next ten years while he lived in Toronto. It ended when Pat moved back to Thailand. Len had kept in touch with Pat and occasionally would ask him computer-related questions via email. Len had ensured that Pat was well compensated for his contracting services to Guthrie Construction. Pat did not forget this. During lean times in the Computer Services business, he could also count on Len to provide him with work. It would be good to see him after all these years.

His phone rang again. It was Karen.

"Pat will you be having dinner with us tonight?"

Pat hesitated. He didn't want to tell them that he was meeting Len. It was supposed to be a surprise visit.

"Is anything wrong, Pat?"

"No, no."

"Are you feeling okay? Are you still in pain after those guys roughed you up?"

"No, I'm fine. Don't worry about me. I just had a call from a friend who wants to meet me this evening."

"Oh."

Pat sensed her disappointment. He wanted to see Karen too. Much nicer company than Len.

"How about I give you a call later this evening?"

"Great, I'd love that."

"We won't go to the harbour though."

Karen laughed. She was happy that she would see him later in the evening and hopefully she could comfort him and provide him a welcome distraction.

Pat hung up. Things could get complicated. Very complicated. He wished he had met Karen earlier in his life. A lot of events had changed him over the years but it had not been for the good. His return to Bangkok had so much promise but things did not work out the way he had hoped. He often wished he had never left Toronto. Toronto the Good.

Chapter 29

"Did you speak to Pat?"

"Yes. He can't make it for dinner but will visit later."

"We need to do something this afternoon. I can't just wait around for the kidnappers to tell us what to do. Maybe we should visit the school again to see if that young student has any information about Carol," said Jessica.

"We can do that but don't expect too much. He may have seen her leaving, but that's all. You've seen how crowded these streets are. There are hundreds of people on the street at any one time."

"And they all look alike, right?" joked Karen.

"And we all look alike to them," responded Jessica.

The concierge phoned for a taxi to take them to the school. He honked frequently, turned onto the wrong side of the road and shouted at pedestrians. They hoped all taxi drivers were not like this one. Jessica turned every time she saw a light-skinned girl with long, dark hair in a crowd of people. The driver screeched to a halt at the school gate, jumped out and opened the door. Jessica paid him and he smiled at the big tip.

"I can wait for you, Miss."

Jessica shook her head. She addressed the gate-keeper. "Hello. I'm Mrs. Guthrie. We are here to see the principal. Can you take us to him?"

"Just a minute, ladies. I will phone Mr. Suttikul's secretary."

He spoke quickly in Thai, nodded and hung up.

"Mr. Suttikul is with other person now. Secretary will phone back when he free."

The school bell rang. It was a break. The students filed out into the compound, well-behaved and polite with no sign of rowdiness. This was a highly disciplined school. Jessica did not recall Carol's school in Calgary having students with such good manners. Boisterous behaviour, shoving, laughing and cursing is what she remembered. This was good to see. However, it was normal for students to minimize unruly behaviour in Thailand. Attending a school was a privilege not afforded to many. Private schools charged fees and poorer students could not afford this, only the public ones, which had a lower standard of education.

The principal's secretary called back to tell the gate-keeper that they could come to the foyer.

"Mrs. Guthrie, Mr. Suttikul will see you now."

She ushered them into his office. He rose up, smiled, shook their hands and beckoned them to be seated in the chairs across from him. He fidgeted with his papers on the desk and was anxious to provide the new information to his visitors.

"Just yesterday I spoke with the young student, Anu Montri. I have some news for you. He had been kidnapped. Possibly by the same persons who took Miss Guthrie."

"Oh. Did he see Carol?" asked Jessica.

"He believes he did see her, but it was from the back, so he is not absolutely certain. He was released in the countryside after being held for some hours. He doesn't know why they released him. Perhaps orders from their bosses."

"May we see this young man?"

The principal asked the secretary to bring Anu. They sipped the tea offered to them while they waited for the break to be over and for Anu to return to his class. Jessica had many questions but she did not want to overwhelm the young boy or to stress him out with her line of questioning. He may not have fully recovered from his frightening experience.

There was a gentle knock on the door and the secretary pushed it open. Anu walked in and stared at these strange ladies. *Which one was Miss Carol's mother?*

Jessica and Karen smiled. A young skinny boy. Not like the others. His complexion was lighter and his eyes were hazel. His hair was brown, not black like the other Thai children. He looked at each of them and quickly looked down. It was impolite to make eye contact for him but he recognized a bit of Miss Carol in Jessica and his heart raced. She was an attractive woman too. Maybe Miss Carol will look like her when she grows up. He stood nervously awaiting direction from the principal.

"Take a seat, Mr. Montri."

Anu sat on the edge of the chair, not wanting to look too comfortable or casual in front of the principal and his important visitors.

"Mr. Montri, Mrs. Guthrie is Miss Guthrie's mother and Mrs. Delaney is her friend. They are here in Bangkok to look for her. I told them about you seeing your teacher with other men after school one day. I have not given them more details about your recent experience. Can you help?" Mr. Suttikul had spoken in Thai. He then turned to Jessica and Karen.

"My student here will tell you first-hand of his experience. His English is good."

"Nice to meet you, Anu," said Jessica.

"You are a brave boy," Karen smiled at him.

Anu shifted nervously in his chair, looked at the wall, with an occasional look at Jessica, Karen and the Principal. He told them about his, and his mother's, unfortunate experience and then the trip in a tuk-tuk to his temporary prison.

"I not see Miss Carol in front, but I see her back and I think definitely it is Miss Carol."

"Did she look alright?" asked Jessica.

"Yes, she walk okay and not seem to be in pain."

"Can you describe the men who took you?"

"Men were Thai. I think some rich man hired them. They not in control. Other men came and talked loudly to them and then took Miss Carol away. Men let me go after that. Just like that."

"So, it appears these men were merely common criminals who are working for someone else," said Mr. Suttikul.

"Are there many cases of kidnappings of westerners in Bangkok?" asked Jessica.

"Sometimes it is kidnappings of local children for money from rich parents. Other times it is poor children to be slaves."

"Sex slaves?" Jessica asked.

Mr. Suttikul was embarrassed. He did not want to volunteer too much information to his visitors about the nasty side of Thailand. He did not want to mention the topic of sex in the presence of his young student.

"I meant that they may be kidnapped to work in fields in the country, or to beg for money for their masters."

Jessica regretted she had asked the question but her thoughts of poor Carol working for violent criminals in a red-light area was entirely plausible. She turned to Anu. "Did you go to the police?"

Anu hesitated and looked at the principal for guidance.

"The police are not very good when locals report kidnappings. They just write a report and don't investigate. I believe this is why Mr. Montri did not go to the police."

Anu nodded.

"Did you go to the police to report your concern about your daughter?"

"Not yet. We have a friend who is helping us with his contacts."

Jessica turned to Anu. "Anu. Thank you so much. You have been very helpful."

Anu smiled. Jessica opened her purse and gave him fifty baht. "Please buy something nice for yourself and your mother. We are staying at *The Metropole*. Maybe you and your mother would like to visit us one evening. We would like to meet her."

Mr. Suttikul quickly said something to Anu in Thai and then turned to Jessica. "I will make sure that they come. I will bring them there when it is convenient for you. We must find your daughter. I also have some police contacts through the school."

Jessica did not want to mention the note that she had received. Things may get too complicated. She didn't want the principal going to the police.

"Thank you, Mr. Suttikul. We will go to the Police office tomorrow with our friend who is hosting us. You have been very kind to arrange this meeting with Anu."

They left the office but Anu stayed behind, and waited for direction from the Principal. He excused him shortly thereafter and Anu ran out. He stopped. He could not say anything further to them and he had to go to class. He saw Jessica and Karen get into a taxi which the gate-keeper had hailed for them. He hoped he had helped. He wished he could have saved Miss Carol when he had the opportunity.

Chapter 30

Len nursed a beer in the hotel restaurant. He liked the local Thai beer. Very different from Canadian beers. *It's all because of the water and it's good that alcohol kills bacteria. I would never drink the local water* he thought. He looked at his watch. Pat should arrive any minute. He looked forward to meeting him again.

"Another beer?"

"Make it two," said Len. It was hot and the humidity in Bangkok was overpowering. What a change from Calgary's climate where there was little humidity, especially at this time of the year. He looked around. *No sign of Pat yet. Why was he late? Maybe the traffic outside. Unbelievable. How could people live in a city like this? Crowds, crowds and more crowds.* He remembered the early postcards he had seen of Thailand. Beaches, palm trees, historic monuments, beautifully crafted pagodas. All he had seen was wall to wall people, pushing, shoving, peddling cigarettes, souvenirs and sex. Len didn't feel good. He didn't look good either, as Pat noticed when he walked in.

"Len! How are you, old friend?"

Len stood up and almost knocked over his beer.

"Pat! Pat! My good friend." He shook his hand and did not let go until Pat gently pulled his away.

"Are you okay, Len?"

"Yes, I'm fine. Just getting hot in here. Want a beer?"

"Would I ever refuse a beer?"

"So, what's been happening?"

"A lot. The ladies are doing fine."

Len's hand trembled as he raised his glass. The room appeared foggy. *Must be too humid in here* he thought.

"Len, you don't look too good. Can I take you to your room?"

He heard Pat saying something but it was unintelligible.

What is he saying? he thought. *Why am I so woozy?*

He stood up and fell over. The beer glasses tipped, rolled over and fell with a crash. Shards of glass were scattered all over the floor. The waiter rushed over. Pat spoke to him in Thai and raised Len to his feet. He was still unsteady. Pat helped his overweight and groggy friend upstairs to his bed.

"Wuz hap'ning?" Len slurred.

"You need to stay in bed for a little while." Pat suspected that Len may be having a stroke. He phoned the hotel Front Desk.

"Is there a doctor in this hotel?"

"I will check." He held onto the handset and hoped that there was a doctor nearby. If this was indeed a stroke, Len needed help immediately. He considered calling an ambulance but then the Operator came back on.

"A doctor is one of our guests and will come to the room shortly."

A few minutes later there was a knock on the door. He let the man in. He was young, very young, may only have been an intern, but Pat had no alternative.

The young man checked Len's eyes, his tongue and listened to his heart. He asked Len to move his right hand and then his left, which Len did slowly.

"Your friend did not have a stroke. It is likely heat exhaustion. He needs to stay in the hotel for a couple of days and drink lots of juices. Call me if there is a problem." He handed Pat his card.

Pat had little experience looking after a sick person. He remembered how his mother would remove his blankets when he had fever. Maybe this is what he should do to Len. Why hadn't the doctor given him more advice? But then why did he not ask himself? Perhaps because he hadn't intended to look after Len. He looked at Len who was breathing

153

hard and sweating. He opened his shirt buttons to expose his chest so that he could cool down a bit. Len was still sweating and breathing hard. Pat put some water in a glass and tried to make him sip but he started coughing. Pat quickly propped him up since he probably got some water in his windpipe. *Not a good idea to give water to someone who is lying down* he remembered a nurse telling him once. He tried again. This time Len gulped some water down. After a few moments he gave him more and continued until the glass was empty. He kept Len propped up, made sure the air conditioner was keeping the room cool enough and went downstairs to buy some juices. He brought these up to Len's room and left them on the table next to him.

"Pat, thanks. I can manage now." Len murmured.

"OK, the bottle of juice is next to you, keep sipping for the next few hours. I will call you in a couple of hours. If you need help right away, call me, or this hotel doctor."

Pat placed the card on the side table and left the room. He was not sure whether he should call Karen now, or wait a couple of hours to hear from Len. He was worried about Len. He was probably over two-hundred and fifty pounds now. Ten years ago, he was at least fifty pounds lighter. The ten years appeared to have done a lot of damage to him. He looked like a prime candidate for a stroke or a heart attack. *This will be messy, if he kicks the bucket while in Thailand* thought Pat. He was not aware if he had any relatives in Canada and if something were to happen here, Pat was his only contact.

"Karen?"

"Yes, Pat?"

"My friend may need help. I may be a little late. Will that be okay?"

"Sure, Pat. Should be fine. I'll let Jessica know."

He hung up. It was important to meet the ladies tonight. There was so much to discuss and they were looking for his help. Now was not the time for Len to be ill. They had a lot to do together. Besides he didn't like to keep the ladies waiting.

Chapter 31

Jessica had not heard more from the kidnappers. She was getting worried. Had they decided to forget about a ransom and instead, taken Carol out to another village to put her to work? Not likely, she thought. Why would they have bothered to leave a note when she was in her hotel room? Someone must have been watching her, and Karen. How did they know which room she was in? In North America, room numbers were not normally given to visitors, instead the desk clerk would phone the room. Maybe it was different in Thailand. Whoever it was may have just asked the clerk and was given the room number. She went down to the Front Desk.

"Did anyone come by yesterday to ask for my room number?"

"You had only one visitor, Mrs. Guthrie. Man you spoke to yesterday."

"That was my friend Pat. Was there anyone else?"

"No, Mrs. Guthrie. I can leave note for other desk clerk if he remembers."

"Don't worry about it. Thank you."

Whoever it was must have followed her from the airport. How did they know when she was coming? The dead crow on her doorstep at home suddenly came to mind. Someone in Calgary had been watching her too, without her being aware of it. The person likely had an accomplice in Bangkok who was advised when she left Calgary. No doubt she had been watched for some time. To ask for a million dollars they must know that she was well off. The professional bounty hunters probably can target just about anyone since so much information is available to internet savvy criminals. When Ben died, his obituary was published. Many business people knew Ben and how much he was worth. Many knew that she had sold Guthrie Construction for a tidy sum. If this was a professional job, why did they bring her to Thailand? They could easily have got some money from her in Calgary. But then, using Carol as bait was a safe bet for them. And bringing her to Bangkok made her more likely to cooperate.

"Jessica, Pat will be a little late."

Karen was in the lobby in her best tropical outfit, no doubt to attract Pat. Jessica liked Pat too, and was pleased that her friend got along well with him. Karen needed someone who treated her well. He ex-husband had treated her shabbily and then ran off with some young, attractive woman who probably wanted his money.

"Okay, would you like to have a drink in the restaurant?"

They ordered Mai Tais. Not really a Thai drink but they wanted something cool, with lots of ice. It was still daylight and the restaurant was not crowded. Tourists were probably taking in the local scene in the outdoor markets.

"We are being watched," Jessica sipped her drink.

"Now? Where?"

"Ever since we arrived."

"How can you tell?"

"It didn't take them too long to find out which hotel we were in, and the rooms we were in."

Karen looked around. A couple of men were seated by the window with their beer. They were tourists with their cameras on shoulder straps or around their necks making them easy targets for pick-pockets and the like. There was another group of six young people who may have been part of a school group, who giggled and took selfies. There were no local Thais in the bar.

"I don't think we are being watched now," said Karen.

"Why haven't they given me further instructions? I was expecting a note this morning. They had been quick in tracking me down and dropping the first note. What's holding them up now?" Jessica asked.

"Is it possible that they saw us visit the principal?"

"Yes, they probably did. But why wouldn't I visit the principal if my daughter was in his school?"

"But maybe they know that you talked to that little boy."

"So what? They let him go, didn't they? There had no interest in the little fellow."

Jessica swirled the Mai Tai around and watched the ice cubes in the glass. She looked at them and hoped that they could be read just like one reads tea leaves in a tea cup. Pat had been so helpful so far. Maybe the kidnappers had delayed him to give him the note. They had, after all, assaulted him previously and told him to pass on a message. Not likely. He must really have a friend in trouble. He was a kind soul who wouldn't let a friend down.

"Should we try to find Jariya Panya while we are waiting for Pat?" asked Karen.

"Yes, let's do that. She had given me an address. I have it in my suitcase in the room."

"Where you want to go, missus?" asked the taxi driver.

"The address I have is 2234 Thoet Thai 20, Bangkok," answered Jessica.

"Oh, that long way from hotel. Not good area of Bangkok. You sure you want go there?"

"Yes, please. I'm not afraid. I have a friend there."

"Ok, missus."

They drove through the modern business areas. Skyscrapers, offices and apartment buildings were more numerous than in Calgary. The taxi went down narrow streets where hawkers sold fruits, live chickens, goats and pigs. People stared at them through the car windows and some came towards them and offered their wares. Bicycles, tuk-tuks and rickshaws now filled the narrow streets. Few cars or taxis were in the area. The cab driver shook his head and apologized to his passengers for the state of the streets.

"Soon we are there. You want I wait for you? Hard to get taxi from here. Not many come here, only rickshaws. You no want to take rickshaw."

He came to a stop outside a row of decrepit apartment buildings. Laundry hung off balconies, dogs ran loose in the street and odours from an open sewer made them question the wisdom of this trip. But Jessica had to find Jariya Panya. They could not see any numbers on the buildings.

"I look for you. I ask," offered the cab driver.

He left the cab, with the engine running and walked between two buildings to ask some urchins who lounged nearby. Between puffs of their

160

cigarettes, they pointed to a building across the street. He came back.

"Want I come with you? Not safe here."

They accepted his offer and walked into the entrance. The numbers '2234' was just visible on the right cornice of the building. There were four separate entrance doors on the main floor.

"What is name of person?" he asked.

"Jariya Panya."

He looked at each door and shook his head. They walked up the stairs to the next floor and the upper floor but none of the names showed 'Panya'.

The driver knocked on one door. An old man came out. The taxi driver repeated the name as he spoke quickly in Thai but the man shook his head.

"Maybe she moved," said Karen.

"Or maybe she was never here," said Jessica "Let's go back."

As they drove away, a pair of brown eyes watched through one of the windows in the building. Helplessly. Sadly. She had strict orders not to speak to any foreigners who visited. If she did, she would lose all the money that was promised to her. She may also lose the opportunity for another promised trip to Canada. Despite that, she regretted not answering the door. Her sadness deepened when she knew she could have helped but had not done so. Her miserable life as a maid in a cheap hotel in Bangkok had been brightened by the hope of some much-needed money and a brighter, more promising future. Being a single girl in Thailand had been difficult.

Jariya Panya had been touched by Jessica and hoped that she would find her daughter, unharmed.

Chapter 32

Anu would not be able to find Miss Carol by himself. He needed some help. But from whom? The principal had offered assistance, but Anu guessed he had an ulterior motive. A donation to the school perhaps by these rich Canadians? Maybe a tip for him too? It would not be the first time that a person in power would use their influence to get some money. Maybe he shouldn't be so cynical. Maybe Mr. Suttikul really did want to help. It was his own school-teacher that was missing. As Principal, he had some responsibility. Maybe he was a moral man after all. Still, Anu felt Suttikul could not do much. A principal who may be wealthy may not have experienced the seedy side of Bangkok. He probably lived in a wealthy neighbourhood and only saw poor people on the drive to work.

That left the police. They made him uncomfortable. But then again, they may know some of the crime rings in Bangkok. Maybe other girls had been kidnapped recently. He walked towards the police station. He hesitated at the gated entrance. A guard stood there.

"What do you want? You can't beg for money inside the station."

"No, sir. I am here to report a missing foreigner."

"A missing tourist?" the guard softened. "Okay, you may go in. The officer at the desk will take your report."

Anu shuffled into the stone building. It was stifling inside. He accustomed to this but not the tourists, who sweated profusely and sipped bottled water. *Bottled water. So unusual for Thai natives. And so expensive.* He would have preferred a Coke, or a Pepsi. The tourists waited on the bench, probably to make a report about pickpockets. He did not want to sit with them, so he remained standing. The desk officer motioned to the tourists to come forward and sit on the chairs in front of his desk. It was a case of a handbag stolen in a crowded marketplace. The officer asked for money and got the usual surprised looks from the tourists. They listened to his justification for the money, nodded and gave him fifty baht. He thanked them and they went away.

He looked at Anu. "Steal anything today?" he asked sarcastically.

"No, sir. I'm here to report a kidnapping."

"A kidnapping?"

"Yes."

"Who was kidnapped?"

"I was."

"Well, you don't look kidnapped right now. Piss off you little shit."

"No, sir. There is another person who was also kidnapped. She is still missing."

"Another urchin like you?"

"No, my school teacher."

"Your school teacher?" the officer did little to hide his sarcasm. "Maybe she was kidnapped by the principal. Ha, ha!"

"No. She was being held in the same compound as I was."

"Maybe she lives there. Go away, I have more important cases to resolve. If a teacher was kidnapped, we would have heard about it from others. People more important than the likes of you."

This conversation was going nowhere. He should never have come. It was a complete waste of time, just as his mother had said. Anu tried to hide his annoyance but the officer sensed it and stood up.

"Get out! You little shit! Don't waste my time!"

The police were there only for the rich people and, of course, the tourists. He left the station and went home. His mother had cooked some fish and rice and they ate together.

"How was school today?"

Anu told her about the meeting with Jessica. He also told her about the principal's offer to help but he didn't tell her about his visit to the police station. She would probably get upset, more so for him trying to get involved in the search for Carol.

"It's good the principal will help. He must have good connections with the police. They will pay attention to him. He is supposed to look after his teachers anyway."

Anu ate his food in silence. There must be another way he could help. Maybe he could find the place where he had been held. He would need transportation. It was a long way. Then again, maybe they had moved Miss Carol to another place. It looked like they were doing that. Kidnappers would often change hideouts to avoid detection. Maybe he would call Mrs. Guthrie at the hotel. She could order a taxi and they could go there together. That seemed to be a better idea. He did not mention this to his mother. Anu remembered that Mrs. Guthrie told Mr. Suttikul which hotel she was staying at. He would call the hotel after school tomorrow and speak to her on the phone.

Chapter 33

Pat called Len but he didn't answer his phone. *Shit! I'd better go over and check on him* he said to himself. He drove over, knocked on the door and heard a groan inside.

"Len, can I come in?"

"Yes."

"Well, can you open the door then? I don't have a key."

He heard him stumble out of bed and the door was opened. He was pale and his skin was slimy. His condition had not changed much. *In his present state Len cannot move ahead with what he had planned to do in Thailand.*

"How about if I come back tomorrow morning, Len?"

"Sounds good," Len grunted. He closed the door and went back to bed.

Pat called Karen. "Karen, how goes it?"

"Good for the moment, Pat. We are looking forward to seeing you again and hope you have some new information about Carol. Will you be coming over now?"

"Yes, be there in fifteen minutes."

What could he do to assist the ladies tonight? Perhaps provide them with a needed distraction from their plight. There were a few good restaurants to take them to, but he was not sure Jessica wanted to enjoy herself when she should be searching for Carol. Maybe he could set up a meeting with his contact. He had suggested this to Jessica previously and perhaps after that they could go to dinner. He called his contact.

"Sunan?"

"Yes. Hello, Pattama."

"Will you have an hour or so this evening to meet my visitors from Canada?"

"Just a minute, let me check." Pat heard him talking to someone in the background.

"Yes, should be okay to see you for an hour or so. Where should we meet?"

"Can we meet at your office, if you will be alone?"

"Yes, can do. See you later, Pattama."

Pat drove to the hotel to pick up the ladies. It was a pleasant evening, not too hot and the smell of jasmine was heavy in the air. Nightingales sang in the palm trees and crickets chirped in the tropical paradise but lots of unpleasant things were on Pat's mind. Jessica and Karen were waiting for him at the front of the hotel.

"Hello ladies, I have my police contact available this evening. He may be able to assist."

"But they told us not to go to the police," said Jessica.

"They always say that, but they know that most people do so anyway," replied Pat.

Jessica did not feel comfortable. "But if this is a well-organized criminal gang, maybe from Russia, this would not be a good idea. I hear they can be very brutal."

"My friend won't be in uniform; he is a plain-clothes detective. Chases down druggies and peddlers. But if you are concerned Jessica, we can call it off."

Jessica shook her head. "No, let's go for it. Maybe I will learn something more about how things work here."

They drove to the less touristy part of Bangkok. Narrow streets were filled with bicycles, street vendors and stray dogs. Small businesses, mainly catering to locals, were located there and all the shop signs were in Thai. Pat was able to park his car near a fire hydrant where some street urchins played in the water that leaked from the hydrant. They entered one of the small buildings and walked up two floors. Pat knocked at one of the doors and Sunan greeted them. He seemed too friendly to be a policeman, thought Jessica, but maybe plain-clothes detectives were supposed to be like very ordinary people.

He ushered them in and they sat on a green vinyl bench seat similar to those in doctor's offices. Sunan sat at a desk across from them. His face was dimly lit by a green-shaded desk lamp. He smiled. "Sorry to bring you to my humble office. Pattama had told me what has happened and I hope I can help in some way. I have some contacts on the street who may have heard which group may be active in recent kidnappings. My contacts play the street scene and see a lot. How long has your daughter been missing?"

"She has not been at the school for the last few days. Got an email from her the day before I left Canada and she seemed okay."

"Does she have a boyfriend?"

"I don't know. She didn't mention one. She had been to Phuket with some friends but didn't mention anyone special."

"Can I see a picture of her?"

Jessica gave him a photo of Carol.

"Pretty girl. I hope it isn't the Russians who have her. They are a bad bunch but they are mostly into drugs. There is also a group from Hong Kong who is very active here. Drugs and prostitution." Sunan got up from his chair. "I have to leave now because I'm on duty tonight. I will let Pattama know if I find anything out. I'm so sorry that you came to Thailand for something like this. There is so much to enjoy here but don't worry, I'm sure things will work out. In my experience they usually ask for a ransom and they don't harm people, especially foreigners. With locals it is different." With that he shook their hands and they left the small office.

"Nice man. Hope he can find something," said Jessica, although she had her doubts since she had got the impression that the man was preoccupied with other things. He did not have the authoritative demeanour of most policemen she had seen, or met previously. Neither had he asked to keep the photograph which he would need to find Carol. His knowledge of English was very good and it was possible that he had been educated in the UK or elsewhere in Europe. *Well, maybe he is one of the higher-ups in the police force who got trained in a foreign country. Possibly an Interpol person.*

They drove back to the more modern area of Bangkok, leaving the poorer area behind them and stopped in front of *The Royal Thai* restaurant. The restaurant was quite busy. Lots of chatter. Most of the patrons were native Thais. Jessica was not too interested in eating. She had too much on her mind. What more can Pat do? When will the kidnappers make contact again? Can the principal do anything? What about the little boy? He must have seen more, or heard more. She would like to talk to him again.

171

Pat interrupted her thoughts, "I will order something for you both. Do you prefer a meat or a fish dish?"

"Fish."

"Same for me," said Karen. "The fish must be good here since it is so fresh."

Pat spoke to the waiter in Thai. He waiter nodded, filled their glasses with guava juice and ice cubes and left.

"So, what did you ladies do today?"

Jessica told him where they had been and Pat seemed to stiffen.

"I thought that would be a good idea," said Jessica.

"That was a risk, going out on your own. Len had asked me to make sure you always had an escort. I feel responsible for you. Please let me take you the next time you want to go."

"We were at the school as well this morning," said Jessica.

"Oh?"

"We met the young boy who had been kidnapped," said Karen.

"A student had been kidnapped?"

They told him what had happened and he smiled. "These little boys always want to be important. I doubt he was kidnapped. He probably wanted to impress the principal."

The waiter brought the steaming platters of food. They spoke little during the meal. All were

preoccupied with the events that had taken place
and what may occur in the coming days. Jessica had
so many hurdles and so many paths to take.
Hopefully one of them would lead to dear Carol.

Chapter 34

Len felt cold and then hot. This was not good. He had come all this way, had so many urgent matters to take care of in a few days and now he gets heat stroke. He guessed he drank too much on the plane. Also, at the Club Thailand or whatever it was called with that Daisy woman, a prostitute if he had ever seen one. Had the heat and humidity given him heat stroke like the doctor had said? He had not been in the sun. Hopefully it was not something more serious, like a heart problem. His father had died of a heart attack in his early fifties but then he was overweight. Len looked at his belly. *I could be following you soon, Dad.* The illness was a kick in the nuts. He had to meet Jessica. Pat had said she was with her friend Karen, someone he had not met.

He sat up in bed, waited for the dizzy spell to pass, stood up and took his suitcase out of the closet. In the pockets were some emergency travel medications which could see him through the next few days. Imodium, Aspirin, Gravol and some Band

Aids. All useless for his present condition. He poured himself some juice and sipped it, burped, and felt better momentarily. Perhaps the sugar or the cold drink made him feel less bad. He took a few more gulps and stood up, walked to the window and looked out.

It was morning. Diesel fumes and smoke began to rise above the roofs of the slum dwellings that surrounded the cheap hotel. The foul air that mingled with the sweat and urine of the inhabitants overpowered the scent of jasmine bushes that lined the streets. Street hawkers began to set up their carts with fruits and vegetables, to be ready for the crowds of locals who would soon fill the street. Sparrows pecked at the lettuce leaves. Rats chewed on discarded banana leaves, unafraid of the vendors. They were doing their job. There were no street cleaners in this part of Bangkok. This was not a five-star hotel. More like a 'no star' so unlike the posh hotels he stayed in when he was with Guthrie Construction. He sighed. How his life had changed. Little did he realize that he would end up in a shithole in Bangkok on an assignment like this. He felt sleepy again. He lay in his bed and saw the ceiling shifting from side to side. He closed his eyes.

It was raining heavily. Len was soaked. He was not prepared for this weather. It was a downpour. The rain in Calgary seemed like a drizzle compared to this. He walked on a bridge. A

very large bridge. Very much like the ones he and
Ben would sometimes build. A stooped shadow of
a person walked towards him. Len heard a call. He
could not see who it was. The shadow took form. It
was a person. He grabbed Len by the shoulders.

"Len!"

It was Ben!

"Ben!?"

How did he get to Bangkok? His hand
reached out and shook Ben's hand thankfully. Ben,
his boss and his only friend. In Bangkok. They were
on a bridge. One that they could have built
together. Ben looked grim.

"Len, what are you doing here?"

"How did you find me?"

"Do you trust me, Len?"

"I will always trust you, Ben. You are my
only friend. How did you get here?"

"Never mind. Len, you've got to pull yourself
together. Leave Bangkok now! Don't do anything
foolish here. You can have a good life back home if
you were to leave now."

"Ben, how did you know?"

"I know you Len, this is not like you. Leave
now. Trust me. Go!"

Ben turned and walked rapidly away from
him, swallowed up in the torrential downpour.

Len awoke with a start. His heart pounded
and he began to sweat again. The room tilted and
he gripped the bedpost to steady himself, stumbled

to the bathroom, and retched into the toilet. A
cockroach, disturbed by the noise, scurried out
from behind the plastic shower curtain. He
continued until he could vomit no more and then
stood up and looked in the bathroom mirror. What
a change! Bloodshot eyes. Blue lips. Veins in his
neck, like worms, about to break through his pallid
skin. He opened the tap and a trickle of orange-
coloured water came out followed by a gush of
yellowish fluid. It cleared up and then he splashed
his sweaty face and neck. The water was not cold
and clean like at home. But it was water. Sort of.
What a shock! It all seemed so real. Ben, of all
people. How he longed that he was still alive. Len
had to call Pat who may not like to hear what he
had to say.

Chapter 35

The class was over. Anu had found it difficult to concentrate and could not wait for the bell to ring so that he could leave. He dashed out of the schoolyard onto the street to look for a public phone booth. Hopefully the booth would have a telephone directory inside. He needed to find the hotel phone number. The Internet at school could have been used but there would be too many teachers present in the room at that time looking over his shoulder, like they would normally do. He didn't want to use his cellphone in case his mother saw what he was searching for. An upscale commercial area where the tourists hung out was not far from the school. There would surely be a public phone booth there. Then he remembered that there was one in the parking lot of a shopping plaza not far from the school. He ran over. *Shit! Someone has taken the directory away.* Only the plastic cover was left behind. Small shops in the plaza included grocery stores, massage parlours, and travel agencies. He would try a grocery store.

Anu walked into one that had reasonably fresh fruit on display outside the shop. The proprietor looked up and then continued to talk to the other customers. Anu could see a phone book behind him on a small table with a telephone.

Good, he would buy something first and then ask. It was too early for mangoes, his favourite fruit, so he selected a couple of custard apples and walked over to the proprietor.

"May I use your phone book please?"

The proprietor eyed him suspiciously. "There is one outside in the public booth."

"No, someone has taken it away."

The proprietor hesitated. He did not trust young boys. They usually stole from his store. This one seemed a bit different. Not aggressive or unruly and quite polite, not like the usual bunch who came to the store for chips and Coke.

"I will look up the number for you but I won't give you the book. I have lost these before. What name are you looking for?"

"A hotel. *The Metropole.*"

"Oh, you have some friends staying at a fancy hotel? Maybe a little American girl?" said the shopkeeper with a pleasant smile.

Anu shook his head. "No, a friend of my teacher who is visiting from Canada."

The shopkeeper wrote the number on a piece of paper and gave it to him.

"Make the call from another phone, please. I can't let you use mine."

Anu left the shop after he paid for the custard apples and called the hotel from the phone in the booth.

"Mrs. Guthrie, please."

"Wait a moment. I will connect you."

He could hear the phone ring and he got nervous. What should he say that he hadn't said before? The phone continued to ring but after ten rings he hung up. She must have gone out, perhaps he would go to the hotel and wait for her to return. This may upset Mr. Suttikul and his mother but he did want to do something to help. He was the one who had seen her being kidnapped and he should have done something at that time. He had to make up for his earlier negligence.

And if she likes me, maybe she will let me marry Miss Carol he thought foolishly. Mrs. Guthrie is very attractive too, like some of the actresses in the movies. Or m*aybe she will adopt me and take me and Mama back to Canada with her.* The foolish thoughts made him smile. Humour was what he needed now. Going to the hotel may not be such a bad idea after all. He must do it quickly though, so that he could get back home without his mother getting too suspicious.

A bus stop was not far away and soon the bus was on the main road to the downtown area with its large buildings, clean streets free of vendors, and manicured gardens. He wondered if Canada was like this. Carol was on his mind again, as she often had been when he allowed his fantasies to take over. His cellphone rang.

"Anu!"

"Mama!"

"Where are you?"

"I'm on a bus going to the city centre."

"Why?"

"The library there is better than the one at school. I need to find a book to research my school work," he lied.

"Alright, but don't be too late."

Shit, that was close, he thought, as he turned off his cellphone.

Anu dismounted in the area where most of the hotels were located. The Metropole was a large twenty storey building set well behind the main street in a large garden courtyard. Guards stood at the gate. *This could be difficult* he thought. However, his school uniform may give him some legitimacy.

"Are you a guest at this hotel?" asked a guard imperiously.

"No, but my principal sent me to meet a teacher who has arrived from Canada," he lied.

The guard had no reason to disbelieve this kid who did not appear to be a trouble-maker. He let him pass. Workers tended to the grounds and did not look up as he passed them. Anu had not been in such a beautiful hotel before and he tried to maintain his confident demeanour as he walked towards the lobby entrance.

Two men dressed in official red jackets and black trousers stood by the entrance. He chose not to look at them in case they misinterpreted his eye contact as seeking permission to enter the exclusive premises. Fortunately, they did not challenge him and the door opened automatically. The air-conditioned lobby provided a needed respite from the outdoor heat. In the lobby he was not sure where he was supposed to go and looked around curiously. He was unaware that the concierge eyed him suspiciously. In a moment another uniformed hotel worker came to him.

"What brings you here?"

"My principal has asked me to meet a teacher here."

"Oh, what is her name?" asked the concierge.

"Mrs. Guthrie."

The man nodded towards the Reception desk. "Go ask the man there."

"The name of the guest?"

"Mrs. Guthrie."

"First name?"

"I don't know. She is a business-woman from Canada who asked me to meet her here."

"Is she expecting you then?"

"Yes, but I am very early." Anu was pleased with his new-found ability to lie glibly. *Amazing what a little stress can do for you* he thought.

"I will call her room." He picked up the red telephone and placed a call. After a few moments he shook his head and hung up.

"Does not appear to be in her room. Do you want to wait for her in the lobby until she returns?"

Anu hesitated. His mother was waiting. "Maybe I will come back tomorrow."

The gaze of the concierge followed him down the path. Something more unpleasant was also following. Someone had been watching him when he entered the hotel and also when he left. Anu walked quickly to the bus stop and hoped he would get home before his mother questioned his long absence. As he waited at the bus stop, a tuk-tuk stopped. *Oh no, its them again! I'm in deep trouble.* He grabbed his cellphone but it dropped from his grasp. He ran as fast as he could to get away but the tuk-tuk that followed him. It caught up with him and stopped. Two men jumped out.

"You little shit! Come here. If you don't this stick will be planted in your head." Anu dove into an alley between two buildings followed by the men. An iron fence, too high to climb over in time sealed off his escape.

"What do you want with me again? I did nothing."

"Why were you at the hotel? Who did you see?"

"No one."

"You little liar!" One of the men grabbed him and held his arms while the other slapped his face several times.

"Liar, why were you there? Tell me, or I will continue until your face is broken. You got away from us once, but not this time."

This is hopeless thought Anu. *I'd better tell them or they will kill me.*

A police siren sounded at the end of the alley. The men stopped and released their grip. He saw his opportunity and ran towards the alley entrance calling: "Police, police."

The men did not follow for a few moments until they were sure the police had gone by. Out in the open street the tuk-tuk driver waited. Anu ran back towards the hotel gate. Besides the guards there were some tourists who were out for a walk. He looked over his shoulder and didn't see any sign of the tuk-tuk and the two men. He began to run again and hoped to leave these empty roads in hotel row and find busier streets where he could get lost in a crowd. Whenever he heard a tuk-tuk behind him he turned to look, but so far it appeared that he was safe.

Appearances could be deceptive.

Chapter 36

"Higginbotham called back. We've got to go to the Royal Bank of Scotland and introduce ourselves. The name of the person we are supposed to meet is Mr. Frederick Lee. Need to take our passports. We can visit the embassy after that."

"Should we ask Pat to come along?" Karen wanted his company.

"No. I don't think our man in the bank would be comfortable with that. Besides, something seems to be troubling Pat. He's not the confident and entertaining person he was when we first met him."

"Yes," said Karen. "I noticed that too. Seems more preoccupied. Could still be tense about the attack. After all, he was just supposed to assist us, not get deeply involved in this matter."

"I'm glad you noticed it too since you have a soft spot for him. I thought I was imagining things. His sick friend may be a girl friend."

"Or maybe his wife. He is too good looking to be single," Karen sighed.

The concierge called them a taxi. Jessica continued to look on both sides of the street with the hope that she would see Carol.

"You want that I wait for you in front of bank?" asked the taxi driver.

Jessica told him he could come back in half an hour. A guard opened the door for them to a large lobby. Marble floors and pillars and the ubiquitous pagoda replicas provided an elegance not seen in banks in Calgary. An attractive Thai lady, dressed in a dark blue uniform approached them with a smile.

"How can I help you?" Her accent was more English than Thai.

"Thank you. We have an appointment with Mr. Lee," said Jessica.

"Oh! You must be Mrs. Guthrie. He is expecting you. My name is Phara." She shook their hands. "Please have a seat."

Her high heels tapped rhythmically on the marble floor as she hurried to one of the large mahogany doors of an office on the far side of the lobby. She knocked gently, opened it, and said something in Thai. She nodded politely and then returned.

"Please come with me. Can I bring you some tea?"

"No, thank you. We won't be very long," said Jessica.

186

Mr. Lee was a slightly-built man dressed in a well tailored dark three-piece business suit, with a white silk shirt and gold cufflinks. He rose to greet them and bowed slightly.

"Very pleased to meet you Mrs. Guthrie. I am Frank Lee." Once again, the accent was more English and less Thai. Schooling in private English schools may be a prerequisite for good banking jobs in Thailand, thought Jessica.

"Thank you. This is my friend Karen Delaney."

"Welcome to Thailand, Mrs. Guthrie and Mrs. Delaney." He shook both their hands and gestured them to have a seat on the red leather chairs as he took his seat behind his large teak desk. Phara smiled and closed the door gently. Her clicking heels could not be heard behind the sturdy door as she retreated.

Mr. Lee's pleasant smile faded as he gave a concerned look to Jessica, waiting for her to lead the conversation. Since Ben's death, Jessica had become more comfortable when she dealt with financial professionals. Being with Ben during some of his business dealings had also been useful.

"Mr. Higginbotham has told you about my circumstances."

"Yes, he has. I am so sorry that you have had such an unpleasant experience in our beautiful city. There is no excuse for this. I am ashamed that some of my countrymen may be involved in this.

Organized crime is not limited to Canada or the US. It is in the most unlikely places."

"It seems to be. I myself didn't know how active it was in Canada, behind the scenes." The heavy traffic outside the large glass window of Mr. Lee's could barely be heard. "The kidnappers have not given me much time. They want one million dollars in five days."

"Yes, so I have been told. I understand that your bank can release only a quarter of the sum in that time."

"I am not sure the kidnappers will accept that. I have not had direct contact with them yet and am awaiting their instructions. These can come at any time. They already know my room number at the hotel. Must have eyes and ears everywhere."

"It appears you are being watched closely. This does not surprise me. They may have accomplices in some of these good hotels."

"Yes, I am afraid so. This must have been a well-planned operation."

"They have probably done this often. Have you told anyone else in Bangkok about this matter?"

"No, I have been told by the kidnappers not to go to the police. However, a local friend took me to see on of his contacts in the police, a plainclothes detective."

"It is good you have a friend who lives here."

"He is a friend of one of my deceased husband's employees. A very helpful person."

"Good." He handed her two pages that had been on his desk. "To initiate the process, I need you to complete this transfer agreement but first I need to see your passport, if you please Mrs. Guthrie."

Jessica gave him the passport and he studied it, made a few notes on his notepad, and returned it to her. He then handed her a gold Parker pen and she read the agreement.

"As you know there will be a fee for this transfer. We are a correspondent bank with the Royal Bank of Canada. Our agreement requires us to charge you approximately five hundred dollars. Normally it is a percentage, but I have been authorized by my manager to limit the fee to five hundred dollars instead. Is that alright with you Mrs. Guthrie?"

"US or Canadian dollars?"

"US dollars, but the Canadian dollar is almost at par with its counterpart at this time."

"That's acceptable to me. When will these funds arrive here for me to pick up?"

"It should not be more than three days. Would you like me to send the money to you at the hotel? I can have a security guard deliver it for you. It is not safe for you to leave the bank with such a large amount of cash."

"That's very kind of you Mr. Lee. I would like that."

"Okay, I will phone you at the hotel when we are ready to deliver it to you. Is there anything else I can help you with, Mrs. Guthrie?"

"Thank you. You have been very kind."

"When the next installment is ready to be sent to us from your bank, I will phone you again."

They left the hotel. The taxicab was waiting outside.

"That didn't seem too difficult," said Karen.

"My difficulties lie ahead of me. The longer I wait the more I am weighed down. Why have they not contacted me again?" She paused. "My God! I hope nothing has happened to Carol recently." She dared not think about Carol being harmed by the criminals due to the delay in acquiring the ransom.

Karen held Jessica's hand tightly. At a time like this no words should be spoken. Eighteen years ago, Karen was at Carol's baptism. As her Godmother, she held her over the baptismal font as Holy Water was poured over her tiny head. That beautiful little bundle of joy, so fragile, so warm and so alive. She must be alive. She had to be!

Chapter 37

The trip to Calgary had been the highlight of her life. An aeroplane! She had never dreamed that she would ever be on one. These had flown over her village many times. Jariya had stopped looking up in wonder at them since she knew that only rich people could fly in aeroplanes. The money she received for the trip would pay for her rent for at least a year. She didn't like the man who accompanied her to Calgary. He said little and kept his distance from her but never let her out of his sight. He had hidden behind a corner of the house while she had visited Jessica in Calgary and she play-acted as she had been told. At first it had appeared to be so easy. Actually, doing it was far more difficult. The tears in her own eyes when Jessica was crying were real. She felt her pain as she had felt her own pain for most of her life. After putting on the show, she was not able to sleep properly and often thought of giving the money back to the man. But that would have done no good. The deed had been done. The crime committed. How she hated herself for that!

However, now that she had seen Jessica again through her window, things were different. She could help. Maybe even expose those who had been so cruel with this plot. There must be others involved but she had met only one man whom she had met in the hotel where she worked. His offer piqued her interest. Travel to Canada! What a dream! All she had to do was to act as if she was in a play. But what an act! What a mistake! She must make amends. Correct the wrong that she had committed.

The hotel where she worked was a cheap one, a bit far from the hotels tourists normally stayed at. After work she planned to visit each one to track down Jessica Guthrie. She would apologize to Jessica. Tell her the truth. Tell her it was a big lie and ask for forgiveness. Offer to pay her back what she was paid for this horrible act.

It was hard to concentrate on her work but she continued to make up the rooms, knocked on each door softly before she opened it. She had to skip one room since the door was locked from the inside and she could hear loud snores. This hotel catered to tourists who could not afford to stay in the more expensive hotels. Mostly the guests were young people in their early twenties from the US, Canada and Europe. After making up the beds she would continue with waitressing duties in the small restaurant. The restaurant was where she had met the man who offered to take her to Canada. She had not seen him since her return.

There were three couples in the restaurant sipping tea. The other waitress nodded to her as Jariya looked after the remaining customers.

"More tea?"

"Please," said the young man, possibly an American. With him was a local Thai girl who did not look up. She was very young, perhaps fifteen.

"Excuse me."

An older man at another table raised his empty teacup and she nodded.

She pushed the kitchen door open and asked the cook if there were any orders ready to take to the customers. He shook his head so she filled two teapots with green tea and went back to the restaurant.

A new customer had arrived. Overweight and pale he sat by himself in a dimly lit area of the restaurant.

"Menu, sir?"

"No. Just a juice please."

"Orange, guava, pineapple or mango?"

"Yeah...pineapple," he grunted.

"You alright, sir?"

"Yes, I'm fine, thank you. Just a little warm."

"Ok, juice will be good for you."

She brought the juice.

"Please bill to my room."

"Yes, sir. Room number?"

"Four two zero."

"Your name, sir?"

"Green, Leonard."

"Green Leonard? OK."

"No. Mr. Leonard Green."

"So sorry, Mr. Green. My English not so good."

Jariya took the receipt and gave it to the cook. She told the cook that she would leave now and he nodded.

She left the hotel and did not realize that she had missed a very important opportunity a few moments ago.

Chapter 38

"Len, are you in there?" Pat knocked loudly at the room door, but there was no answer. No sound came from within the room, no snores, footsteps or running water. Pat went downstairs to the reception area.

"Is Mr. Green in?"

The clerk picked up the telephone.

"No, I was just up at his room. He didn't answer my knocks."

"Did you check the restaurant, sir?"

Pat's eyes adjusted to the darkened restaurant. To save electricity cost was another way to cut overhead in the less expensive hotels. Len sat by himself, looking at his glass of juice. He looked up when Pat entered.

"Pat! I'm here."

Pat came over and shook his hand.

"You're looking good. Got some sleep?"

"Some. Still a bit woozy but much better than yesterday."

195

"Are you okay if I get things moving for you? The guys are getting impatient to see you."

Len hesitated.

"Well?"

He said nothing and took another sip from his glass and looked around the restaurant nervously.

"Len, you've come a long way. You've invested a lot in this trip. You need to do something here. Maybe you need to rest some more. Maybe clear your mind and think things over."

Len looked away, took another sip and fumbled with his paper napkin.

"Yeah, maybe I do need some rest. Let me call you in a couple of hours."

Pat was silent. *Shit! This guy is all screwed up. Why did I offer to help him? I've set everything up for him. Organized everything he has to do and now he wants to sit on his ass while the world turns!*

He got up quickly, nodded to Len, and walked out of the restaurant.

Len signalled the waitress. "A beer! No, make that two."

Ben was right. I've got to go home. Bangkok is not right for me. It was never a good idea. Len sipped on the golden ale. The recipe for this beer may have been passed on to the Thais by the British. Drinking alcohol was not a good idea at this time. He knew it, but he didn't give a damn.

Bangkok would be a memory soon after his plan to make an early return. *But what about Pat? How should I tell him? Should I tell him at all? Would I really be missed if I left?* He took another gulp of beer, bubbles dribbled down the corners of his mouth. *Just like the old days. Drinking beer with Ben after work.* The restaurant was getting darker. *Where is the waitress? They really need more light in here. Oh no! Another dizzy spell. Gotta get up to my room and lie down for awhile.*

"I need help," said the waitress to the cook. "A guest has passed out on the table."

After getting a key from the desk clerk at Reception, the cook and the bus boy helped Len back to his room, put him on the bed, closed the door and hung a 'Do Not Disturb' sign on the doorknob.

The room phone rang. Len could not hear it. His sleep was deep. Just as well for him.

Chapter 39

Anu was not far from his home now. What would he tell his mother? He had to tell her he was in danger again. Someone had to know. A taxi passed him. The taxi was followed by a tuk-tuk with the two men who had pursued him. They jumped out and grabbed him. He kicked one of them in the shin but the man only grunted and punched him in the stomach. This was followed by a sharp slap to his face. "Don't you dare do that again!"

He was pinned in the tuk-tuk by the two men, who pushed his head down so that he could not see where he was going. One of them covered his mouth and nose with his hand. Anu struggled to breathe and felt he would pass out. The tuk-tuk picked up speed but he could still hear cars, rickshaws and cyclists. Every now and then one of the men would shout at him. "Why weren't you at school today?!" He knew that the man only did that to pretend to be his father in case anyone saw them. The traffic slowed and he let his body go limp. One of the captors assumed he had fallen unconscious so he loosened his grip. Anu elbowed them both in their groin. They grunted in shock and released him. He stumbled out of the slow-moving tuk-tuk and ran on the pedestrian pathway of a bridge. Both men jumped out after him to give chase. Cyclists rang their bells and taxis blew their horns as the two men dodged the traffic. Few paid any attention to the young boy who ran along the pathway. Anu ran off the bridge and followed the riverbank. A forested area by the river bank would be reached within a few moments. The men still pursued him and did not seem to tire as he expected them to. A path through the trees provided some hope and he made for it. After a few minutes on the path, he turned left among the trees and ran as fast as he could. The men passed by and shouted to each other. After a few moments, he turned around and ran in the direction he had come from... right into the arms of the tuk-tuk driver! Anu kicked and bit his hands but the man would not let go. The driver shouted to the others who returned. One of them slapped him a few times as he tried to kick him in the shins.

"Now we have you, you little shit!"

"Don't try any more stunts like that, or you will get this." The other man showed him a knife. Anu felt that these men would kill him and think nothing of it. They escorted him back to the bridge where the tuk-tuk was parked just off the roadway.

"Any screaming while you are with us and you get this stuck in your ribs. Your mother will only get your head after we cut it off." He was squeezed in between the two men and one of them showed that he still had the knife in his pocket, ready to be used. The tuk-tuk jerked forward and Anu grunted as he felt a stab in his thigh. The knife man grinned at him, obviously pleased by the little 'accident'. Things could get more serious if necessary. The wound hurt and his pant leg was soaked with blood. He pressed down on the cut with the hope that the bleeding would stop.

"Little boys who know too much can get hurt. Hurt very badly," the knife man said. "We wanted you to stay with us and would have let you go. But no, you think you will make us look stupid with our boss."

"Ha, when he meets our boss, I am sure he will want to kill him right away. He has no time for stupid boys. If you were a girl, he may take you someplace nice, where you can entertain tourists. He may have done that with you but now that you have shown you are a runner, I think he will kill you," said the tuk-tuk driver with a laugh.

"Quiet! Do not frighten the boy. We may need him too. His mother owns a shop so she must have some money."

"But he is not worth much. Maybe his mama won't come looking for him." The conversation stopped when they came to the country road which continued for a few kilometers until they arrived at the building he was held in previously.

"We will not be giving you any food tonight. You have been bad and will be punished," the knife man said.

"You will not be left alone again, not even for a moment."

They pushed him into the same room and slammed the door shut. It was padlocked from the outside and the two men went back to their chairs by the gate. The tuk-tuk's sound faded in the distance as it drove back to the city.

Anu listened for sounds from the room above, but there were none. They must have moved Miss Carol to another place. But where?

He should have been more concerned about where he would be taken to.

Chapter 40

"Another day without a word from them," said Jessica.

"Maybe they know that it takes time to get the money sent over. Everyone should know that Jess, even here in Bangkok. They probably move even slower in this place."

"Maybe, but I just can't sit around here while Carol is in trouble. I want to do something but don't know what. If we are being watched there's not much I can do, except to find out who is watching us. And maybe grab them by the scruff of the neck and kick them in their balls."

"Maybe we should ask Pat if we can call his policeman friend. He could have heard something in the meantime."

"If he had, he would have told Pat, who would have called us right away."

"Pat may still be having a problem he doesn't want to talk about. Maybe he knows something that we don't."

"What do you mean?" asked Jessica.

"Maybe his contact has told him something about Carol he doesn't want us to know just yet. He is less talkative lately, almost brooding."

They were sitting on the restaurant patio and watched as the traffic went by and kept a lookout for Pat's car. The sound of buses, tuk-tuks and police sirens no longer bothered them. Neither did the fumes from all the exhaust pipes. Hundreds of vehicles. Hundreds of people. Totally unlike Calgary which would almost be like a cemetery compared to this place.

"He should have phoned me by now. Do you think he is married?"

"Does he think you are married?" Jessica laughed.

"What if he doesn't call, or show up? Should we go to the principal again tomorrow? Maybe he can take us to see that young lad."

"Mrs. Guthrie?"

It was the bell hop. "I have note for you. Urgent." He gave her an envelope and she gave him a tip.

Jessica opened the envelope.

"What does it say?"

Jessica was silent, reading the note again.

"I can't believe this."

"What? Another threat? Instructions?"

"No. It's from Jariya Panya."

"What?!"

"She was here. Look what she wrote."

Jessica read the note *You came my apartment. I not come out. I very sorry cause so much trouble for you. Did not mean to hurt you. Bad men gave me money. Say not talk to you if you come. Should not have taken money. Will come back later.*"

"Just as I thought. They used her to lure me here! Bastards!"

They left some money next to the bill on the table and left. The concierge told them that a young woman had been there fifteen minutes ago. They had called Jessica's room and there was no answer so she left them a note to give to her. The woman had said it was very important that Jessica receive the note soon, so the bellhop had gone to look for her. Since she was not in her room and he had not seen her leave the hotel he came to the restaurant.

"Maybe we can go look for her. She can't be far away."

Karen's phone rang.

"Pat! Jessica just had a visitor." She told him about the note and hung up.

"He's coming over shortly. He said we should not leave the hotel."

A bus arrived at the hotel entrance. Several American tourists got out and started to fill the lobby. They all talked excitedly. A few moments later Pat jostled through the crowd. He led them to his car and started to drive away from the hotel. He looked grim.

"So, you had an interesting visitor...she will probably be back looking for money."

"You seem to be annoyed," said Jessica.

"Pardon me. It just irritates me that there is so much begging in this city. They even have the audacity to come to the hotels now. Security here must be poor, allowing them in."

"But it was Jariya Panya!" Karen said.

"Maybe, maybe not. It could be one of the kidnapping crew looking for some extra money before the main loot comes in. Don't meet with these people alone. Make sure I am with you when you schedule a meeting."

"Suppose they want me to come alone? Most kidnappers do not like other people. Besides, they may think you're a cop!"

"We expected to hear from them by now. What could be wrong?" asked Karen.

"Don't know. Could be many things," muttered Pat.

"Where are we going?"

"To my place for now. I don't want that woman coming back to bother you. I will phone the hotel and tell them they should not let prostitutes in to bother the guests."

"Why would you do that Pat?" asked Jessica. "Jariya is not a prostitute and I want to meet her."

"It is not safe, Jessica. Believe me. I know Bangkok. There are some nasty, nasty people here. I don't want you to have more complications. You have enough on your mind now."

"No, Pat. I want to meet Jariya. I have to see her. She could lead us to Carol."

"Lead you?! She could get Carol killed!"

Jessica was shocked by his anger. "Pat! You are getting a little carried away."

Pat pulled the car over to the side of the road.

"I'm so sorry I said that, Jessica. It has been a tough day for all of us. I am so angry that those guys have done this to you. I'm trying to help, but am getting too emotional. I know that getting Carol back is our top priority. It has to be done as quickly as possible. I can't bear the thought that some woman shows up posing as someone who wants to help you. She could put Carol in danger." He started the car again and nosed into the traffic. His mind was in turmoil.

What a mistake! How can he show anger when he is supposed to help Jessica? He's got to keep calm. The women have confidence in him and it was important to keep it that way. What about Len? How is he doing now? He hadn't called like he was supposed to. This had to end pretty soon. The longer it drags on the worse it will get.

"When did the banker say he would have the money?" Pat asked gently.

"He was expediting it but we can get only a quarter of the amount within five days. I need to negotiate with the bastards to allow me more time."

"It may not work."

"What else can I do? The bank manager has started the ball rolling but transferring so much money in a short time requires government bureaucracies to get involved and approve. Things are harder now because of the attention being paid to money laundering and cyber crime."

"Yeah, I guess so. If it was a corporate transfer, it would have been easier. With a personal transfer I imagine he is right."

They drove in silence until they arrived at a neat row of apartments in an elegant area. Pat pulled into his underground parking and led them to the elevator. A security guard opened the door for them to the lobby area. An elevator operator, a young boy, smiled at Pat and greeted him. Cheap labour appeared to be in abundant supply in Bangkok.

"Welcome to my parlour," Pat had opened the door and guided them to his living room.

"You are a very neat bachelor," said Karen.

"I have someone who comes in every day to keep it clean and tidy."

"You also have good taste in furnishings," said Karen.

"Well, to be honest, the apartment was furnished. I am renting. I wouldn't know how to select good furniture. Travel around too much on business. Never settled down."

"You need to settle down sometime, Pat," said Karen.

"I am still young, only twenty-nine."

"Yes, and I'm twenty-one," Karen laughed.

The balcony where they were seated overlooked the central courtyard. Parrots squawked loudly in the banyan trees while the gardener tended to the flower gardens.

"Lovely place."

"Thank you. What can I bring you to drink, ladies?"

"A cold beer would be good."

"Make that two," said Karen.

Pat nodded and returned with two foamy glasses of beer.

"I have some bad news, Jessica."

Chapter 41

Footsteps on the cobbled path approached the doorway. The lock was opened and the door pushed open. Anu's two kidnappers entered and smiled malevolently. A third man was dressed in a suit and wore Rayban sunglasses. He stood farther away.

"He will do. Tie him up." He reached into his jacket pocket and took out a few hundred baht and gave it to the kidnappers. They smiled, nodded their thanks and began to tie Anu's hands behind his back. They also tied his ankles and put a blindfold on him.

"Throw him into the trunk," said the man in the suit. He was lifted like a sack of potatoes by the two men and put into the open trunk.

"Let me out!" Anu screamed.

"If you keep shouting, I will throw you into the river. Do you want to live or not? If you want to live, be quiet and I will take care of you. If not, you can scream, I will stop and throw you off the bridge. If you want the river, say so now. If not, shut up. Is that understood?" the man said in a deep voice.

Anu chose to remain silent, and hoped to escape again when the opportunity arose. The car sped down the bumpy dirt road. He expected to be in the city soon, the sooner the better. It was hot in the trunk with no air movement. Sweat ran down his face and soaked the blindfold but Anu did not dare to call out to the driver who, without a doubt, would stop and throw him off a bridge as he had threatened to do. Lives, especially those of children, were lost every day in Thailand. There were many children of destitute parents that were available for whatever evil their masters had in store for them. It was possible he would be taken to a place where he would be enslaved or made to beg on the streets for his master. Bangkok would be the preferred location for him but he knew that this would not be likely. There were other towns far enough away from Bangkok where they may take him.

Anu's journey was made more miserable by a foul smell in the trunk. This may have been food that had been forgotten or perhaps a dead animal that had been transported at one time. Hopefully it had not been a corpse of a young boy. There was no part of the journey so far on a paved road so he knew that his destination would be a remote town or village. He thought of his mother and Miss Carol and the happiness that they had given him. For a moment he hoped that Miss Carol would be at the same place he was being taken to, but he knew this was not likely. It was good to have that hope though. He would be more than delighted to see her alive and well.

The car began to slow down and the ride became bumpier. Rhythmic bumps meant they were driving over a bridge. The car stopped and a door was opened and closed. He heard the man walk away and heard some voices in the distance. The trunk was opened. He was pulled out and carried on someone's shoulders for a short distance. The cries of babies and other voices could be heard. He was dropped on a floor and his blindfold removed. A stout Thai man scowled at him.

"Stay where you are."

Through the opening of the shack, he could see young children talking to each other. What he did not see was the fence around this compound and the guards at each gate. The guard returned with leg irons. The rope that bound his hands and legs was cut with a large sharp knife which the man handled skillfully. He knew what he would do if Anu made any quick movements. Leg irons were put on and he was told to stand up and given some water in a tin mug.

"You can go out now but not too far from this hut. The master will be here to talk to you. Do not disrespect him. Other boys who did have had their legs cut off. You don't want that, do you?"

He laughed and then walked away into the bright sunlight. Anu hesitated but needed to get out of this little hut. His leg irons hung loosely on the top of his feet and allowed him to take only very small steps. In the yard there were smaller children, boys and girls without leg irons. They looked to be four to six years old. Some stood at the chain link fence and looked out at the village which was a kilometre away. The area was large, possibly a few acres in size, and all fenced in. There were three small, two-storey white buildings with little windows in the middle of the compound. He noticed three foreigners leaving these buildings; older men, possibly in their fifties or sixties. They walked past him towards the main gate. One turned and looked at him.

"Aha, some new blood. That's what we need in this place."

The other two laughed and walked on towards the main gate. A guard opened the gate and was given some money by each of the tourists. A taxi waited outside to take them back to the city.

"Bastards."

Anu turned around. It was another young boy but without leg irons.

"You know what's ahead for you, don't you?" the bitterness not hidden in his tone.

"I suppose. Prostitution?"

"I have been here for two years. Tried to escape three times and got beaten with whips. Kept in confinement for three days. No food, only water. My name is Jamie."

"Anu. I live in Bangkok with my mother."

"You won't see her again. My father sold me to the Head Bastard here without my mother knowing. Don't try to escape too soon, but try anyway. You won't live past fifteen. No boys older than fourteen remain here, only the girls."

"Where are the girls?"

"In those buildings. The last building is the brothel for the boys and the other two are for the girls. You see these four-year-olds? They take them too. The foreign bastards will screw anything that moves."

"Are they American?"

"Some. They also come from Russia, Saudi Arabia and European countries and Canada. Any country where there are rich people. The Head Bastard is the worst. He screws boys and girls. Used to be a cop. Some of them help him run this place."

Suddenly Jamie turned and walked away.

"Hey you!" Anu turned to see the man who had brought him here. He was accompanied by two others.

"We need to talk about the rules of this place. Follow me."

To speed him up the two bodyguards grabbed him under his armpits and took him to a smaller shelter, which looked like a guardhouse. They pushed him onto a small chair. A large man with a beard and a mustache stared at him. *This is probably the Head Bastard* Anu thought. He went behind a desk and pulled out a large brown ledger. Without looking up he took a pen and started to write.

"What's your name?"

"Anu."

The man slapped him hard across his face.

"Your name is Frederick. We will call you Freddy for our customers. You will not leave this compound." He looked up and glared at Anu. "Did you hear that?" he snarled while he moved his face which almost touched Anu's.

Anu nodded, "Yes, sir."

"You will do what I say!" He turned to the guards. "Leave me alone with him for a little while. I need to teach him how to behave with our visitors.

After the guards left, he told Anu to drop his pants. The initiation began and Anu refused to cry out as his tormentor molested him for what seemed like an hour or so. Some time later the Head Bastard called for the guards.

The guards dragged him back to a hut and threw him on the floor. "Enjoy your stay!"
He lay in the dirt for some time and waited for the pain to subside. *It was unbelievable what the man had done to him. And this was what was probably happening in this place all the time to all the other children. Why had nothing been done? Where are*

the police? Who cares for the kidnapped children?
He would never tell his mother about this. He had to
get out of this place. Soon. But how?

Chapter 42

"Mrs. Guthrie, please."

"She is not in. She does not want to see you. Do not come back to bother our guests or we will call the police," said the hotel receptionist to Jariya.

"But why?"

"I do not know and I don't care why. Her host called us to tell us that he did not want any of your type coming here to see her. Is that understood?"

Jariya was crestfallen. Her only chance to make amends was gone.

"Can I leave a note for her?"

The receptionist hesitated. This woman's pleading voice sounded so much like his sister's. She had died in the tsunami. There should be no harm to accept her note.

"Here is a piece of paper and a pen. Make it quick before her host returns."

Jariya sat on a ledge by the window, rather than on the luxurious sofas in the lobby, and began writing her message. A few moments later she returned and gave him the folded note, and thanked him for his kindness. The man grunted, took it from her and put it in the pigeon hole for Jessica's room. After she left, he removed the note, shredded it and threw it into the wastepaper basket.

She did not walk to the street entrance. She chose instead to walk towards the back of the hotel. A security guard watched her closely to make sure she did try to steal anything from the guest cars that were parked there. He followed her from a distance until she disappeared down the slope towards the river.

A rock close to the river's edge was a good spot to sit and soothe her troubled mind. The pain she had caused Jessica hurt her more than ever before. She had been complicit in the lie just for money and had ignored her conscience. But she had needed the money. There was so little left over after she paid her rent and bought food. Jobs had been hard to find and the hotel work, with its low pay, was all that she was able to get. The hotel supervisors hardly smiled when she asked if there were any waitressing positions available. Some had even been rude and told her that they would only hire young, attractive women. She looked too old. She didn't smile enough. They told her that she should have looked for a job as a cook in a kitchen. The nasty remarks made by prospective employers hurt her deeply. She was too ashamed to go back to her old parents in her village to tell them that she had failed to get a good job. They expected so much of her. She was going to bring them lots of money from her job in the booming city of Bangkok. She knew that other women were employed in the sex trade and did not tell their parents. Jariya did not want to disgrace her mother and father by considering such a profession.

The man who offered her a trip to Canada was like an angel at that time. It was a time when she was most depressed and his offer had come at just the right moment. All she had to do was to meet someone in Canada and tell them a story. She would not know the person. It would have no impact. It was just another rich person. *So what?* she had said to herself at that time. Little did she know the impact her play-acting would have on her. Her nights had been troubled. Jessica's soft, kind eyes haunted her sleep. She needed to make amends. To tell the truth and to accept the consequences.

The strong current tugged on the riverbank and pulled small pebbles which rolled and disappeared into the dark water. Some were held by the stout roots of the large bodhi tree. She had loved trees as a child and would climb any tree to try to catch the little songbirds that nestled in their branches.

The river now smelled of roses as she gazed into the eddies that appeared and disappeared close to the bank. Foam that churned up by the pathways, through the pebbles, billowed into clouds of vapour which took forms that were human and sometimes animal. Waves lapped against the shore and caressed her feet. The water felt warm, like the milk from her mother's breast. Her mother looked down at her and hummed that familiar children's folk song that put her to sleep. The smell of roses was stronger now, as the warm wind blew their gentle scent down the riverbank. She was alone. Alone with the river. The same river that flowed through her village. The river where she had learned to swim with her father. Later in her childhood they would float down in a small boat and would eat mangoes and guavas. She felt she was in the boat again and was a happy child once more. She danced as her father played his flute. The river gave her peace. It renewed her life, which had been broken by her dishonourable behaviour.

"Hello."

Jariya looked up. It was an old man. She was not afraid. She had seen him many times in her dreams. He was a kind man and also a wise one. In her dreams he would give her hope for her future. He was her angel.

"Is something troubling you, my child?"

She hesitated. "Yes." She did not want to lie to her angel.

"Can I help you?" he asked with a gentle smile on his face. Why had she not noticed his presence before this? It was almost as if he had come out of the water!

He stepped towards her and she put out her hand which he took gently into his own, soft hand. "Don't worry, little one. Life can be hard sometimes. I will make it better." She felt light-headed and stood up. The old man's face waxed and waned in the fog but the smile remained. A soothing, loving smile.

"Come with me, little one. Don't be afraid." She followed him into the water. It was warm and her spirits lifted. They walked hand in hand. The river cradled her like her mother had done so many years ago. The rhythm of the waves gave solace to her damaged soul. It was so peaceful.

The old man smiled, one arm on her shoulder while the other held her hand in his, just like her father did when he had taught her to swim. They continued as the water rose to her breast. She could hear the soft tinkle of bells. The tinkle grew softer with each step. The old man's presence gave her comfort which she needed so much. Especially at this time. His face was now hidden in the mist. She felt a coolness and felt his presence. She was at peace, as she floated effortlessly in the river. Peace. Peace at last.

Jariya Panya's body washed up on the river bank the following day. Far from the city and even farther from her cherished childhood home.

Chapter 43

Len woke with a start. He had heard something. It may have been the telephone. Probably Pat. It was five in the evening. He rubbed his eyes as he got out of bed. There was no more dizziness. Likely, the sound sleep had relieved his condition, whatever it was. There were things to be done here in Bangkok which could not be delayed any further. The puffiness in his face was reduced and some colour had come back to his pale skin. *Should he call Pat, or just drop in at his apartment?* He had the address. A surprise may be in order. Then again, maybe he had company and would not like anyone to drop in just like that unannounced. Best to call first.

He dialed the number. The ringing continued six times until Pat's voicemail intercepted asking him to leave a message, which he did.

"It's Len. Let's get together this evening." He hung up. He did not want to leave the room in case the phone rang. He took a closer look at the

221

pictures on the wall. A painting of a pagoda and another of boats on a river.

"You will be a great artist one day," his Grade Six Art teacher had told him. She had been a good teacher, one of the few he had really liked. The other teachers did not treat him as well, and made the odd nasty remark about him being overweight for a young schoolboy. 'Play football.' 'Join the Track team' were some of the cutting remarks they made to him. Maybe he should have kept up his Art. He would likely have been quite successful selling his paintings. But then again, he enjoyed his work with Guthrie Construction, especially with Ben. It was odd that Ben appeared in his dream and said those things. An omen. Ben had often given good advice on a professional and a personal level.

He straightened the pictures and studied them more closely. The colour of the water in the river was different from paintings he had seen in Canada. He had usually made water bluer in his own paintings. Of course, here it was muddy. Muddy rivers didn't appeal to him. Lots of people and lots of boats disturbed the banks with their trees and bushes. Interesting, he thought. A fast-moving city and a fast-moving river. He needed to pick up his pace too, didn't want to stay too long in Bangkok. Two days was more than enough already but he knew it could be longer. A lot of money had been spent on this trip. Money which he didn't have. The credit card bill would be due next month. But then things could go well in Bangkok and he would be out of the red soon, he hoped.

The black telephone sat there in silence. He willed it to ring but nothing happened. *Time is being wasted* he thought. *Maybe he should go to Pat's apartment after all.* He had exchanged Christmas cards with Pat and knew his address. He thumbed through the notebook that he had brought along '1500 Rangsit Road, Bangkok.' He checked his pockets and had everything he needed. A city map, his wallet, his Swiss Army knife (which he had got from Ben), a hotel business card, in case he forgot the name of the hotel and of course, his notebook. With his hand on the doorknob, he glanced again at the telephone which did not cooperate with a ring in response. He closed the door, took the stairs to the lobby and checked again with the Front Desk in case Pat had called. He hadn't, so he asked for a taxi to be called.

"Where you go, sir? Girlie show?"

"No, 1500 Rangsit Road."

"Oh, that not in commercial area."

"No, it is a friend's apartment."

"Oh, friend. A nice Thai girl maybe?"

Len was getting irritated. But an older man, travelling alone, usually was expected to seek out girlie joints or prostitutes. "No, it is a business associate."

"Sorry, sir. You look like rich American man. They go to bars or red-light area. Lots of young girls in Bangkok. Make money from Americans. You from America?"

"No, Canada."

"I no tell difference. So sorry."

You can say that again thought Len. He hadn't liked some of the projects he had done in the US. Usually, they ran over budget because Ben's American clients were too picky and squeezed the most out of contractors. Canadian businessmen were careful too, but they would make sure they would not bankrupt you, so they always cut some slack in their dealings, especially when they dealt with Canadian companies. Seemed like a Brotherhood.

They were outside the commercial area and travelled along a very scenic road by the river. Bangkok's high-rise buildings cut a magnificent silhouette against the gray sky. He wondered what their main money-maker was in Thailand. He assumed it was tourism but that alone could not create such a well-developed infrastructure which he could see. The purpose of his visit to Thailand did not require him to do any research about the country. His stay would be short he hoped, but things do not always go as planned. He knew this from experience.

Missing in Bangkok

Little did he realize how poorly he had planned the trip. He would find out soon. Very soon.

Chapter 44

"He has been kidnapped."

"Many young boys go to their friend's homes, play computer games, forget so much time has passed, forget to call their parents," the police officer said as he looked at the distraught woman across his desk.

"But he always comes home after school! He didn't yesterday," she said.

"But Mrs. Montri. I too have a son, same age as yours. He often goes to his friend's house and stays there overnight. Young boys do that these days. He must have friends in school that he visits. Sons don't always tell their mama where they go. They may have secrets."

"No! He has no secrets from me. He is all I have. You must help me. He was kidnapped before, but he escaped. It is likely the same two persons who did it before. They came to my house and bound me while they took him away. After he was gone for a half hour or so, the other kidnapper freed me of the ropes but told me not to call the police or my son would be harmed."

"Do we have a file on the kidnapping?"

"When he first reported it, your officer didn't believe him and sent him out of the station."

Sergeant Chan was sympathetic. It was no secret that the police paid little attention to the poor people. They were paid to protect the businesses and the rich people in Bangkok. Those who could afford to pay taxes and would be generous with 'tips'.

"Just a moment. Would you like some tea while I speak to my superintendent?"

"No, thank you. I will wait for you."

Chan nodded, gave her a warm smile and went down the hallway. She heard him knock at one of the large brown office doors.

"Sir, sorry to disturb you. May I speak to you for a moment?"

Superintendent Panichkul looked up from his computer. "What's it this time? A prostitute in trouble again with the tourists?"

"No, it is a woman. A mother. She believes her son has been kidnapped."

"And he did not run away?"

"No. They had a very good relationship. He was the only child. The father was a tourist who is no longer in Thailand."

"Oh! Interesting. A hit and run?" he laughed. "Oh shit!"

"What sir?"

"I just screwed up. Lost another game. I will never beat this computer at Chess. It is much too smart. Now you were saying there is a woman at your desk who has lost her daughter."

"Son. She believes he was kidnapped." Chan new that his boss had been on a porn site and not playing chess. He didn't hide the racy magazines on his desk, some of them had been banned in the country but somehow his boss had acquired them.

"Kidnapped, eh? How long has he been missing?"

"Since yesterday."

"Only yesterday? And she is worried? Tell her to come back tomorrow if he is still missing, or maybe day after tomorrow."

Sergeant Chan did not move away but stood and twisted his cap. "He was kidnapped before."

"Oh, and she paid a ransom and got him back?"

"No sir, he escaped. They must have caught him again."

"Tell her to come back tomorrow. If he is still missing, make a report."

Sergeant Chan turned towards the door.

"Go! Tell her!"

He closed the door gently behind him and walked slowly to his desk. The unhappy woman had to be sent away. The way all these poor women were sent away. Given some false hopes, but police had other priorities. There could be rental cars stolen from tourists or another stabbing in the red-light area.

"Can you come back tomorrow if he is still missing?"

"No. He is missing. I will not leave until you do something. He is all I have. You must help me!"

"But..."

"I know a reporter. TV station from America. He comes to my shop."

"You will disgrace your country?" Chan asked severely. He was however, nervous about Western reporters. A story of prostitution and child pornography recently appeared in a New York paper which his boss had seen on the Internet. He was furious. Tourism must not be hurt by stories like this, he had said. Now this woman wanted to talk to a reporter.

"I want my son. I will do anything to get him back. If you police can't help, I will get help from outside." Tears streamed down her face as she got up to leave.

Chan was taken aback. He didn't want this woman making a scene in the lobby. There were other westerners there. Bad for business in Bangkok.

"Sit, sit. Give me the details."

Taneka had surprised herself. But now she was acting for Anu. Her son. Her treasure. She was not fighting for herself, but for him. He was in grave danger. She would not return home empty-handed. She wanted action.

He took out his pen and she told him what had happened. How men had broken into her apartment, tied her up and taken Anu away. She gave a description of the men but nothing significant which she could remember. No scars, tattoos or any other distinguishing remarks. There were lots criminals in Bangkok, just like in any other city.

He put down his pen and looked at the poor woman. "Come back at nine o'clock tomorrow. I will work on this case myself and will ask some questions of the street constables. Promise me you will not talk to any reporters before then."

She nodded. "He is all I have. He is a brave boy and may try to fight them. They may kill him."

He led her out through the lobby to make sure she did not speak to any of the tourists waiting there. He opened the door for her and smiled. "This is a very difficult time for you. I too have a young child. I worry about him a lot." With both hands he squeezed her hand gently. "Don't worry, we will find him."

He watched the poor woman walk away, back bowed with her recent loss and probably the weight of many previous hurts and tragedies. So many women, young and old, suffered in this city. They suffered because the wealthy took all and gave back little. He remembered his own mother, stooped and going to work everyday at the dry-cleaning shop. She left early and came back late, smelt of perchloroethylene (perc) used in the business. Chemicals which were being phased out in Western countries but were still used here, with poor ventilation and little regard for the health of workers. His mother had died young at age fifty-five, of cancer. No doubt the chemical had caused this. Mrs. Montri's gait reminded him of his dead mother. Another poor woman left to fend for herself in the big city. She could have stayed in her village and would have had a happier life, but the bright city lights of Bangkok had so much promise for village people. For him too. He was lucky he thought. His father had stayed on in the village and Chan would send him money. He found out early that his low salary could be supplemented by occasional 'gifts' from tourists whom he had helped. This was not really 'illegal' and was more like a 'tip' for services provided. No guilty conscience here. Tourists had lots of money to spend. They knew the rules here. Tipping the police was common. He was certain the superintendent was getting a lot more, in his position, from some powerful businessman.

The man was a good politician and knew which businesses he should respond to quickly. He was however, concerned about the Western press publishing stories about Thailand being a haven for pedophiles. Chan himself was getting nervous about this. Hence, he cautioned Mrs. Montri not to speak to reporters. It was possible that her son had been kidnapped for this purpose. He intended to check with his contacts on the street about villages outside Bangkok dedicated to providing prostitution services to foreigners. It brought good money into Thailand and provided the villagers and the police with a good living. He had never been to one of these places but it would not surprise him if his superintendent had some contact with these criminals. He should, however, remind him that it was time to perform a raid for the benefit of the Western press. They did this occasionally after forewarning their contacts about imminent raids. The key people would get away, and a few of the workers would be put in jail for a few months. The superintendent likely got paid off for warning the top guy. He did not like this. Not at all. When he had joined the police force, he had been an honourable man. Corruption was rampant in some precincts. Especially those close to the red-light areas. He could not help being corrupted. *It wasn't his fault* he thought. He had to make a living, like everyone else.

Mrs. Montri was about to turn a corner. Her head seemed to be jerk, likely with sobs. Poor woman. Chan was going to help her.

Chapter 45

"What is the bad news, Pat? Is it about Carol?" asked Jessica.

"Somewhat," replied Pat. I had a visitor this afternoon."

"Oh?"

"He knows where Carol is."

"Where?"

"Outside Bangkok, is all he said."

"What else did he say?" asked Jessica.

"That's what surprised me. He told me that you need to stay here, in this apartment, until he returns."

Something was odd thought Jessica. "How did they track you down?"

"It is not difficult. They know that I am with you sometimes and they must have been following me."

"But why didn't they come to me directly?"

"Because the hotel is not the place where they want to do business. Too many people, too many guards."

"Did he tell you when he would return?"

"He was going to phone me."

"Phone you?!" asked Jessica.

"Yes, I had to give him my number. It's less dangerous for you. I don't want them threatening you."

"What did he look like?" asked Karen.

"A local. A Thai. Not a foreigner. But then again, the person, or persons, pulling the strings could be foreigners. Tough to say. He was fairly confident. Seemed to know exactly what to do. Not a mere messenger, but likely one of the key people on the team. Let's have another drink until he calls."

"Not for me."

"Me neither, this is not the time for drinks," said Karen.

"Not to worry ladies. This should work out fine if we play our cards right."

"If I play my cards right." Jessica did not hide her annoyance with Pat. *He really should have let them know about this earlier. Why did he wait until they were in his apartment?*

"We are in this together, Jessica. I made a promise to Len that I would take care of you. In Thailand I will look after you until we get Carol back."

"I really don't want to wait here, Pat. I'd rather be in the hotel. They could just as well call you there and tell us where to meet them."

Pat hesitated. "But they may be nearby already. Maybe the guy is waiting around the block. He probably saw us come here. If we leave, he may get upset and tell us that the deal is off."

"I just don't have a good feeling about this. They could quite easily have left a message at the hotel, just like they did previously. You should have told them to call me, or Karen. We are always together and her room is next door to mine."

A car could be heard stopping in the parking lot. The car door slammed but Pat assumed it was a visitor for one of the other tenants. He froze when someone knocked on the door. "Let me check this out. I wasn't expecting anyone, just the phone call." He was not happy that someone should show up at a time like this.

He opened the door. "What are you .... Len! Come in!"

Len grunted and came in the door and looked at Jessica and Karen. He seemed taken aback but quickly regained his composure.

"Jessica, Karen. This was supposed to be a surprise for later," said Pat. He was not comfortable.

Jessica jumped up and greeted Len. "Len, what brought you here? Pat has been taking good care of us. This is Karen. I don't believe you have met her before."

"Nice to meet you, Karen," he shook her hand. "I'm here on business with Pat. He told me about some opportunities in Thailand for someone with my experience." He turned to Pat. "I tried calling you and couldn't get through."

"I understand, Len. No problem. Have a seat."

"What happened?" asked Jessica as Len slowly sat down. He appeared to be in pain.

"Probably a bug, although the hotel doctor said it was heat stroke."

Pat's phone rang. He spoke quickly in Thai and then hung up.

Jessica and Karen looked at him questioningly. "Was that them?"

"No, it was someone else. I will talk to them later." Pat had now regained his composure and acted as the good host again.

"So how are things going?" asked Len.

"Not good. Carol's kidnappers want one million dollars in ransom. We are waiting for the funds and waiting for the next instructions from them."

"They contacted me recently, Len." said Pat.

"And I don't see why they did," complained Jessica. "They had sent me a note before, so why contact Pat now? Something is fishy."

"They did rough me up, Jessica. As I said, it was easy for them to find me. They also want to make sure I'm not with you for the exchange of Carol for the money. They don't trust me," responded Pat as he poured Len a beer.

"Do you blame them?" Len laughed.

"That's not funny, Len. Pat has been a very good guide for us here. He was almost shot when I was with him," said Karen.

"You have another bodyguard?" asked Len.

"Another?" queried Jessica.

"He is thinking of the chauffeur I used to have when I first moved to Bangkok in a well-paying position," said Pat.

"So, it's not a female bodyguard..." Karen looked inquisitively at Pat.

"There have been other things that have been happening, Len." Jessica told him about the schoolboy who had been kidnapped and then released.

Len seemed shocked. "Why would a schoolboy be kidnapped as well as Carol? Were they together at the time?"

"No, not together, the boy was kidnapped later. He may have seen the kidnappers," Jessica responded.

"Is he back home now?"

"Yes, we met him at the school. He seemed okay," said Jessica.

Len shifted uncomfortably and looked at Pat. "This is not good. I hope Carol is safe."

"She should be," answered Pat. "The kidnappers want Jessica and Karen to stay here until the money comes in."

"What is the reason for this?" Len was now agitated.

"Don't worry, Len. We can take care of ourselves. We don't plan to stay here. They told Pat that the hotel is too public. That's why they want us here," said Jessica.

"You know what?" asked Pat. "Let me drive you back to your hotel now. If they come here, they will meet Len. Len, can you stay until I return?"

"Yes, I can handle this."

Jessica turned to Pat and then to Len. "But Len, we don't want you getting hurt on my account."

"I can look after myself. Go with Pat. Don't worry."

Jessica did not get up from her chair. "I don't want to miss an opportunity to get this over quickly. I will stay, but Karen can go back."

"No way! If you stay, so will I," said her friend.

The men looked at each other. "Umm, the kidnappers may not like to meet with all four of us. Even if there may be only two of them, they are likely to run off if they see four of us together."

"Well then, all of you can leave and I will stay until they return. I want proof that Carol is safe and I want to tell them that."

"They can take you away too," said Karen.

"Good! As long as they take me to Carol. But then if they take me, how will they get the money, huh? Go, I will stay."

Karen did not rise to leave. "I can't go and let you stay by yourself, Jess."

"Len, maybe we should let the ladies be here for a couple of hours. We can go somewhere and return. They can call me on my cellphone."

Len grunted in agreement and got up. "Okay ladies, we won't be far away."

"There's munchies in the fridge if you're hungry. Make yourself at home," Pat picked up his car keys, opened the door to let Len out. "Take care. See you soon and don't worry, I'm sure Carol is alright."

"Well. What's going to happen now?" asked Jessica.

"They want the money so I'm sure we'll see them soon, or hear from them." Karen opened the fridge and grabbed a celery stick. "Want one?"

"No," said Jessica. "A baseball bat instead of a celery stick would make me feel more secure."

"Kidnappers here don't normally get violent, Pat had said. All they want is money from rich tourists."

An hour or so went by and the phone didn't ring. Jessica was getting restless.

"C'mon assholes. I want my daughter back. I will have the money."

"We have company," said Karen as she saw a car in the parking lot and two persons getting out. "This could be them."

Shortly thereafter there was the sound of footsteps close to the door and then there was a knock. Jessica opened the door to see a man with a bandana covering part of his face.

"Mrs. Guthrie?"

"Yes."

"You have money?"

"No. I will be getting it in two weeks."

"Two weeks too long. What is problem?"

"Can't transfer so much so soon."

"Not okay. We need some money sooner or your daughter will get hurt."

"If you prove my daughter is alright, I will arrange for some in the meantime."

"What proof do you want?"

"I want to see her."

"No. Not possible."

"How do I know she's alive?"

"You will get proof, when you give some money soon. I come in two days. Come here. In night. You wait here. No men must be with you. We are watching you."

"I need proof before I get the money. I need it today. Understand?"

The man laughed and walked away to his partner who sat in the car with the engine running.

"Assholes," muttered Jessica.

Chapter 46

"Why now?" shouted the superintendent.

"Because the woman may go to an American reporter. She said she would if we didn't help her, so I told her not to do so."

"What!? The bitch wants to go to a reporter on her own? Ha! They won't listen to her."

"She is very determined and won't wait long. Her son is all she has. No other children."

"She's lucky. Children are a pain in the ass."

"We really need to show her we are doing something."

"I know. Well, I will organize a raid. Let me work on this."

"Can I help?"

"No, I have contacts. I will let you know."

Chan stood but made no attempt to leave.

"Go!"

"But sir, can this be done soon? She will be back tomorrow."

"What's with you? Do you have the hots for this bitch?"

"Sir, she is an older woman but I think she may go to the school and speak to the principal. He may phone the Police Chief."

"Shit! Okay, go. I will get things moving." He reached for the phone as Chan opened the door to leave his office.

An hour later the Superintendent called Chan to his office. "We go there this afternoon. Two police cars with the reporter's car in between us. He is a Canadian. They are always bugging us since the shooting of one of their citizens by that stupid policeman."

"Where are we going, sir?"

"To the same village I went to two years ago. It is the only one close to Bangkok and likely has that boy. I called the local village police and they will meet me at the entrance."

"I should tell the woman of our plans."

"No. Don't you dare do that! We could get into trouble."

"What trouble, sir?"

"You ask too many questions! Leave this to me. Be ready for this afternoon. Don't tell that woman. If we don't find the boy we will be in more trouble. She will talk to some reporters or that principal. I can't have that happening in my district. It is one of the best run places in Bangkok."

Sure, thought Chan. *The best run district. Can you imagine how the other districts are run?* Chan shook his head and left the office. He was pleased however, that something was being done but suspected that there had been a lot going on behind the scenes that he was not being told about. His boss had connections. Not all the right ones. But he did get results when the heat was on.

The public had a short memory. Lots of pictures would be taken with the superintendent who relished good publicity for himself. He was also well connected to the local municipal officials and had received some awards for policing by the Chief of Police. This was a nasty business. Money gets things done. Important people knew how to control the events that made the city look good.

Chan opened his lunchbox and took out his meal. Always the same. But his wife was a good one. Not good looking, but she got the housework done and her cooking was good. Munching his food, he opened the newspaper and scanned the City section. There was the story again.

Parents Unhappy with Slow Response by Police. This was the couple that the Superintendent had mentioned. Their son had been shot by a police officer who was still on the job. 'No inquiry had been held' was a line in the story. *What a joke* he thought *What is an Inquiry? If someone gets shot that's the way it is. Why is an Inquiry needed?*

"Let's go!"

It was one of his fellow officers. He left the remains of his food and quickly got up and put on his hat. This would be a good photo opportunity. Maybe he would get into the picture this time.

The superintendent was already in the lead car sitting in the back seat and looked very imposing. Another rental car waited in the lot and he saw two Western men who were probably reporters. The lead car gave the signal and they pulled out of the lot. He noticed that a man in the car in front of them already had his video camera on his shoulder, not wanting to miss any important footage. These foreign reporters were very pushy. Always got their way. The boss knew how to keep the local reporters under control by just giving them the big stories on the police successes. But these foreign reporters had too many connections locally and they usually got their way.

"We are off to the devil's den again," said his colleague who drove the car.

"I've never been to that. What goes on there?"

"You've spent too much time in the city. You need to get out of Bangkok and find the real criminals. The bastards who run sex camps with little children. The lowest scum. Make our murderers look like saints."

"Don't they have their own police in the village?"

"You do really need to get out, Chan! Those assholes are on the payroll too. Do you think a village policeman can make any money in a small town of four hundred people? What do you think brings in all the tourists? The nice village scenery? It's a sex camp for tourists. Stuff that their own countries don't allow. But here it's a big money maker! Fucking little children! The whole fucking village lives off this! Lots of money to be made. The kids get fed, have nice accommodations, get fucked a few times a day and then continue to play! They don't know any better!"

Chan snorted. "Despicable. We should shoot the whole bunch who run the camp."

"That won't happen. The main guys are not at the camp." He looked at Chan and laughed. "Maybe our boss has a piece of the action too."

"He is not that bad."

"Do you think Panichkul is that good? The son of a bitch hasn't got us a raise in three years! He probably thinks all of us are on the take like he is."

Chan said nothing. Best to say nothing. He too was guilty of accepting 'gifts' every now and then. His colleague was probably mad that he could not get gifts as lavish as his boss probably got. He pulled out a packet of cigarettes and offered one to his colleague. "No thanks. I only smoke the good stuff," the man laughed. Chan lit up and smoked in silence as his colleague followed the two cars. They had been out of the city for almost an hour when the lead car started to slow down. The reporters in the car ahead scrambled to get all their gear ready and expected lots of fanfare with this raid. A small white car pulled out of a dirt road and a man got out.

The lead car stopped and Chan could see his boss talking to the man. He was dressed in khaki clothing which may have been all the village could afford for a uniform. He did not appear to be carrying a gun. In the villages this would be unnecessary. The reporters started to get out of their car, but Panichkul stuck his hand out and told them to get back in, which they did after they shot a quick video clip of the surroundings. The small white car drove slowly first and then started to pick up speed. Through the dust they could just about make out the form of the car ahead. After a few minutes of driving the cars pulled into a gate and they saw men scrambling to get away from the compound. Chan and his colleague jumped out and gave chase to a couple of the men and brought them down. Panichkul's driver opened the car door and his boss got out and looked around imperiously as the reporters jumped out with their cameras running. The footage of this impressive superintendent would impress many overseas viewers.

"That white building first!" yelled Panichkul. The commotion in the compound brought some of the young residents out and they stood silently while the policemen approached. Chan felt an evil presence in the surroundings. He had heard about these places but had never seen them. Small children, some only four years old, were alone in the rooms with only a bed. Some looked up fearfully. Others held their hands out expecting candy. An older white man appeared out of one of the rooms and tried to run outside but was grabbed by Chan's colleague.

"Leave me alone. I'm just a visitor," the man yelled.

"Sure," said Chan as he handcuffed him.

Other foreign men started to come out into the hallway trying to squeeze past. The reporter stuck a microphone near the mouth of one of the tourists.
"What are you doing here, sir?"

The man tried to hide his face and didn't respond. All the others looked away as the camera approached them but none tried to run because there was only one road out.

"Bring them here," said the village policeman. "I will make the arrests here!"

Chan looked at his boss who nodded his agreement. The men were led away outside the compound.

"Where are they going?" asked one of the reporters.

"He will take their names and some information," replied Panichkul. "They will be dealt with according to our local laws."

"They are under arrest then?" persisted the reporter with his cameraman zeroing in on Panichkul.

"They will be severely dealt with. But we are here first to rescue these children. Our men need to make a thorough search of the premises. Make sure that all the children will be taken away from here and reunited with their parents."

The men began to search all the rooms in the building and asked the children to go into the compound where they were lined up to be interviewed by the police.

"Your name?" asked Chan.

"Anurak Montri."

"When were you brought here?" Chan tried to hide his pleasure at finding the boy whom he had come here for.

"Yesterday."

"Would you be able to recognize the person who brought you here?"

"Yes. He picked me up from another house where I was being held prisoner. I believe he purchased me from my captors."

"Oh?"

"I believe the same persons who kidnapped me took my teacher too."

"Your teacher?!"

"Yes. She is from Canada and has disappeared. Her mother is looking for her and has come to Bangkok."

Chan was really excited now. This was indeed going to be a great catch, if he could also find the teacher.

"Do you think she may be here?"

"I don't know. I haven't been out of my room since I got here. I did see her, from the back, when she was taken from the building where I was held prisoner at another place."

"Her name?"

"Miss Guthrie. Carol Guthrie. At school we call her Miss Carol."

"Come with me. We must search all these buildings in case she is being held here."

Chan and Anu began to search the large building first. There were many rooms but they were now emptied of their occupants who were all in the courtyard. Children of various ages. They searched for hidden rooms by tapping on the walls and calling 'Miss Guthrie!' After searching all three buildings it was clear that Carol was not at this place.

"Well, young man. Your mother will be very happy to see you."

"Is she alright? She has had a very difficult time. They had kept her tied up when they took me the first time."

"That is what she told me. It is because of her persistence that we are all here. Your mother is a real treasure." Chan showed his soft side but changed his tone, to be more official.

"Okay, wait for me at the gate. We will start taking everyone to the station."

One of the reporters approached Chan. "What have we here?"

"A young boy who was kidnapped yesterday."

"Were you harmed in any way young man?" asked the reporter.

Anu hesitated. He did not want to tell them about what the Fat Bastard had done to him the day before. It would hurt his mother too much. The damage it had caused him was bad enough. "I would have been if I had been here any longer."

"Perhaps the boy should not answer any more questions," intervened Chan "he may still be in shock."

The reporter backed away looking for others to interview or film. Anu headed to the gate with the other children. A group of twenty who had been used by tourists for their amusement. Also, a source of much needed tourist money for the nearby village. And, of course, some other corrupt officials.

Chapter 47

An hour had gone by. Jessica paced the apartment and waited for something to happen. It had to happen now. Pat and Len had not returned yet. She hadn't expected them to. Pat's apartment phone rang and Jessica tensed up. Karen hesitated. "Should I pick it up? It may be a personal call for Pat or it may be the kidnappers."

"Maybe it's Pat. Pick it up."

Karen lifted the receiver "Hello.... Hello?" There was a click and then the dial tone. "Maybe a wrong number," said Karen.

"I don't think so. It could be the kidnappers, making sure we are still here." Jessica steeled herself for the next ring.

The phone rang again and Karen picked it up "Hello..."

"Mrs. Guthrie?"

"No, this is not Mrs. Guthrie"

"Need Mrs. Guthrie. Now!"

Karen hesitated. "Jessica. They want to talk to you." Karen held the phone out to her. Jessica's skin became cold, her breathing became more rapid and her knees were giving away. She quickly sat down.

"I can't."

"Mum.... mum, please.... help me!" Jessica heard the voice clearly coming through the earpiece. It was Carol! She tried to stand but fell to the couch again. Karen rushed over to hold her while she trembled. A few moments later she stopped. The fear had subsided.

"Thank God! My baby is alive!"

The phone rang again and Jessica picked it up. "You have proof. We need money. Tomorrow!" The caller hung up.

"They called to tell me that I have the proof and they need the money tomorrow," said Jessica. "Bastards! I've got to get the money from the bank in the morning. Phone Pat and tell him its OK to come back now."

Karen nodded and called Pat's cell. He answered promptly. "They are on the way."

Karen opened a beer and offered it to Jessica.

"No, thanks. I need to think clearly. There's a lot to do tonight and tomorrow. Need to make some calls."

"Right now?"

"No, when we get to the hotel."

"We could make it from here."

"I'd prefer not to," said Jessica.

"Do you think the phone is bugged?"

Jessica hesitated. She didn't want to tell Karen her real concern. Not now anyway.

"Could be worse than that."

"What do you mean?"

There was a knock on the door. The men were back. Len was breathing heavily.

"Maybe I should have stayed here," said Pat. "What did they say?"

"They want the money tomorrow."

"But you don't have it yet, right?" asked Pat.

"They think I do. And that's all that matters to them. They have Carol."

"Did you believe them?" asked Len.

"She was on the phone. I heard her."

"Did she sound okay?" asked Pat.

"She seemed afraid," Jessica said as she moved towards Karen on the couch. The phone call was disturbing but it was a relief that Carol was alright.

Karen put her arm around her shoulder. "I think we should go back to the hotel now."

"Yes, there's a lot to do tomorrow."

They left the apartment and went towards Pat's car. Jessica and Karen sat in the back and Len took the front seat.

"Would you recognize the man if you saw him?" asked Pat.

"No, he wore something on his face. He is a local. Spoke enough English to get his point across," said Jessica.

They stopped at the hotel entrance and Pat jumped out to open the door for the women. "What time should I pick you up in the morning?" asked Pat. "Ten o'clock good?'

Jessica jumped in before Karen could say anything.

"No. We will call you. Need to make a bunch of phone calls tomorrow to raise the money more quickly."

Pat hesitated. "I can try to get a loan for you."

"A loan?! For that much money?!" asked Jessica.

"Well, part of it anyway," said Pat.

"Don't worry, Pat. You've done more than enough. If I need a loan, I will let you know."

"OK, take care, ladies!" Pat and Len drove off into the night.

Jessica looked at her watch. "We are thirteen hours ahead of Calgary. It's night here, so it must be morning there. Banks will be open now. Let's start at the bottom, Higginbotham..."

They went to Karen's room and gave the number to the hotel operator.

"He'd better be there... I don't have another contact in the bank who can help in this instance."

"We have your party on the line now, Mrs. Delaney." Karen gave the phone to Jessica.

"Hello, Royal Bank of Canada."

"Long distance from Bangkok for Mr. Higginbotham please," Jessica said.

"Higginbotham. Is that you Mrs. Guthrie?"

"Yes, it is. Do I have to prove it?"

"No. I have your hotel phone on Call Display."

"Can the full amount be sent? Have you looked at options to get it sooner?"

"I have been making further inquiries of my contact in Bangkok. We can extend a loan guarantee from your account and they can take care of getting the money. You will have to talk to the same gentleman you met."

"Oh, that's great news."

"Just a minute. I want to caution you about going through with this. You really should be going to the police. Have you told the Canadian Embassy yet about Carol being missing? Also, the Royal Bank does not want to know the details of the transfer of money from the bank in Bangkok to you. It is not something we get involved with on the ground, so to speak. It's really none of our business. All we want is the guarantee and we can consider taking equity in your home in Calgary. This would be good collateral for the loan."

"Ok. I assume we can meet that guy again at the Bank of Scotland here."

"Yes, that Mr. Lee fellow."

"That's right. He seemed like a nice man," said Jessica.

"Most bankers are, Mrs. Guthrie. We have to be nice. People trust us with all their life savings, right?"

"Thanks a million, no pun intended. We will visit Mr. Lee in the morning. Please email him to let him know we will be visiting and that you and I agreed on the collateral. Our time is running out."

"Will do, Mrs. Guthrie. But please take care. I sincerely hope Carol is safe and will be returning with you. You really should report this to the embassy or to the police."

"Yes, we might do that. Thanks, Mr. Higginbotham!" Jessica hung up. "Whew! What a relief! We will have the money tomorrow."

"I hope it all works out. Now we have to think of how we can hide a bag with that much money in it."

"Maybe Mr. Lee can give us larger notes and possibly a suitable bag which won't arouse suspicion."

"If we are being watched it may get taken from us," said Karen.

"I'm sure bankers can give advice on how best the money is given to us." Jessica was not worried. She had handled large amounts of cash before. Not a million, but a few hundred thousand at a time.

"Let's get some sleep. Hopefully tomorrow will be our last day in the city and we can head back to Calgary with Carol."

256

"Bet on it," said Karen as she opened the door to let Jessica out.

Chapter 48

"I spoke to Mr. Higginbotham. Perhaps there is something that we can do here in Bangkok. It is not our usual practice but Mr. Higginbotham has given us a guarantee and we can advance you the funds you require. We also feel that you should be going to the police with this case."

"I can't. My daughter's life is in danger," said Jessica.

"Understand, Mrs. Guthrie." Mr. Lee opened a leather-bound portfolio on his desk and studied it for a few moments. He looked at Jessica and Karen and then slowly rose from his chair.

"Our bank is in a difficult position, Mrs. Guthrie. To loan such a large sum of money to a foreigner who has no permanent residency will normally require authorization from the Ministry of Finance. There is a lot of concern in our industry about money laundering, especially with the thriving drug industry. Our bank cannot be embarrassed by something like this. I have taken

Mr. Higginbotham's word about your reputation and good standing in Canada. As such I have alerted the Ministry to the situation. Since kidnappings of foreigners in Thailand are not usual, I was given permission to loan the money to you to ensure the safe return of your daughter. I have assured them that you will call me when you have your daughter back. Can you contact me when she is with you again? I need to give this information to our government. The kidnappers can act again on another foreigner. We can't have our Tourism Industry hit by such a scandal."

"Yes. Certainly. I will let you know. I am sure tourism is very important to your country's economy," said Jessica. *But my daughter is far more important to me than your industry.*

Mr. Lee sat down again. "It is important. But there are many other industries which are larger. We do however, want to maintain our reputation of being a safe place for tourists to visit."

Jessica was about to ask about the sex trade in Thailand but wisely did not speak. "I am not comfortable with taking such a large amount of money at one time. Can you give me some suggestions on how best to do this without attracting too much attention?" she asked.

"Yes. We can have it delivered to your hotel by someone who looks like an airline agent. He will come to the hotel with an ordinary looking suitcase. He will ask the receptionist to call you so that you can sign for your bag which arrived late. The bag will have an Air Canada tag on it."

"Oh, that sounds easy," said Jessica.

"It should not attract anyone's attention. Once it is delivered to you it will be your responsibility for safekeeping. If it gets lost or stolen, I will not be able to advance you any more funds, even with a guarantee from your bank." Mr. Lee reached into his coat pocket and took out a gold cigarette case. "Can I offer both of you a cigarette?"

"No thanks, we don't smoke," said Jessica.

"You don't mind if I smoke?"

"Not at all," Jessica was thinking what else she should ask Mr. Lee while she was here. Should these be unmarked bills, or should they be marked? She had heard about dyes one could put on the bills but it usually was the police that did that. It would be too much to ask this bank to do that. Besides one million was a small amount to pay for Carol's return.

"When can it be delivered?"

"Tomorrow morning. I will ask our people to put the money in the suitcase." He reached into his drawer and took something out. "Here is the key for the suitcase. Don't lose it. I don't have another one."

"They wanted the money today. I will tell them they have to wait. They shouldn't object to one more day."

Mr. Lee rose, came around his desk and shook hands with Jessica and Karen. He held Jessica's hand with some sincerity. "I hope you get your daughter back, Mrs. Guthrie. I have a daughter too. It must be so difficult for you. I am so sorry that you have come to our great country to experience something like this."

Chapter 49

The superintendent was pleased. He had come back to the station after phoning one of his more trusted local reporters to tell them that they had completed a successful raid. He got out of his car to be greeted by cheering reporters. He smiled proudly for their clicking cameras. Chan followed behind and kept a discreet distance from the Press. His boss needed to bask in the glory. He walked over to the area where the small bus had just stopped and guided Anu and the children into a back entrance of the station. Chan had also been careful to phone Taneka Montri prior to leaving the village since he felt a special responsibility to her. He had maneuvered his corrupt boss to finally do something and was not keen on introducing Anu or Taneka to him.

He led all the children into the police cafeteria and told them that they could eat whatever they liked. Many were thrilled to see some real food, having become used to the subsistence diet they had been fed which consisted of lentils and rice. Occasionally some fruit had been given to them. Chan gave instructions to the staff to watch over the children for a few moments while he went to his office. He asked his assistant to get other officers into the cafeteria to interview the children so that their parents could be located. While he did this, he entered the front lobby.

Taneka rose quickly as Chan entered. "Where is he?"

"Come with me," he said as he led her to the cafeteria. Anu ran over to her and threw his arms around her. He did not cry but held his mother as she hugged and kissed him, crying with joy.

"Thank you, Officer Chan! You are a hero," she said.

"Just my job, Mrs. Montri. Would you like some tea?"

The cafeteria had a festive atmosphere. Children talked excitedly while they gobbled large plates heaped with pieces of meat, potatoes, rice and noodles. Soft drinks were guzzled by all. To anyone entering it may have seemed like a children's birthday party. Taneka and Anu sipped their tea while the rest of the children stuffed their mouths and dribbled rice and noodles on the table.

Anu was happy to be back with his mother and glad to see that the children were now free from their oppressors. His mind was still on Miss

Carol. He wondered where she was, and what he could do to help find her.

Chapter 50

"Karen, I got a call from the kidnappers to ask if Jessica has all the money. They want to give directions where to meet."

"Just a minute, Pat. I have to talk to her." Karen put her cellphone on mute and knocked gently on Jessica's room door. There was no immediate response. "Pat, can I call you back?" She hung up and knocked again. "Are you in there?" After a few moments she decided to go down into the lobby.

Jessica was there at the Front Desk, signing for her suitcase. Karen smiled and walked over.

"The delivery person didn't want to give the suitcase to the concierge so he came and knocked at my door to bring me down. These Airlines are really careful these days, aren't they?" said Jessica as she winked at Karen and looked at the Air Canada luggage tag. "Yup, this is mine alright."

They went to Jessica's room and opened the suitcase with the key she had been given by Lee.

Stacks of bills in various denominations were packed in. There was also a note from Lee. *Mrs. Guthrie. I have personally supervised the money count and it is correct. However, you should satisfy yourself too, by counting it. Please be careful when dealing with those people who have your daughter. I hope you get her back. Sincerely, Frank Lee.*

"Let's do it," said Jessica.

"I've never counted a million dollars. I wish I could call this fun. Jess, I am so unhappy for you. I hope you are doing the right thing by paying these criminals."

After checking that her door was firmly locked from the inside, she put the security chain through the latch, came back to the suitcase and emptied the contents onto the bed. She pushed approximately half of it to one side and asked Karen to count that side while she began to count the stacks and place them back into the suitcase.

"We have it all. Carol is worth much more than this to me," said Jessica without any regret in her voice. "We have to discuss the exchange with them. I want Carol first before the bastards get the suitcase."

"Should I call Pat now to tell him we have the money and to ask them to call my phone?"

"No. Just tell him to tell them to call me. Say nothing about the money. What's to stop them from barging in here and taking the suitcase from me at gunpoint? I have to figure out a safe exchange."

Jessica sat down at the room desk for a few moments. "OK, ask Pat to tell them to call your cellphone. I've got an idea."

Karen nodded and made the call.

After giving Pat the message, she paused, while he talked.

"No, Jessica doesn't have the money with her but wants them to call on my cell." She hung up the phone and sat next to Jessica.

"I wish we had some strong men with us. I'm beginning to get a bit scared."

"I will act like this has happened before. When they call, I will take my time in responding. Will pause frequently. That will make them nervous," said Jessica.

"Is that really a good idea? They may think we have the police listening, trying to trace the call," replied Karen.

"I have a gut feeling that this is the first time these guys are doing this. Real kidnappers think much farther ahead and have everything planned carefully. If these guys were pros, they would have put a lot more pressure on me."

Jessica shoved the suitcase under the bed, making sure her own suitcases were clearly visible if someone barged in. She left her purse on the dresser just in case.

Jessica jumped when the phone rang even though she was expecting the call. She let it ring three times.

"Hello."

"You have the money?"

"Umm... not right now," she paused. "Not all of it, but I can get the rest soon. But you need to send me a photo of Carol now, on this cellphone and I will let you know when you will have the money."

There was a pause on the other end. She could hear voices in the background speaking Thai.

"OK, but soon," said Jessica and hung up.

They waited half an hour before the phone beeped. She opened it and saw a message was waiting. There was a picture of Carol sitting on a sofa in an apartment.

"Good. Let's download this photo to a computer. I need to see a larger view. The cellphone screen is too small to pick up any details. The hotel must have one for guests to use."

"Why do you want to do this?" asked Karen.

"You'll see. Wait in my room just in case someone tries to get in. Will be back shortly. Phone the Front Desk if anyone tries to get in and tell them someone is trying to break into the room."

Jessica went downstairs and asked if she could use a guest computer. The receptionist asked the concierge to show Jessica the room where the guest computers were located.

"Checking emails, Mrs. Guthrie?" asked the concierge as he opened the door to the computer room.

"Yes."

He left her and closed the door behind him. There were two computers in the room and no one else was there. She connected the cellphone to the computer with the cable. She knew how to download or upload pictures since she had seen Carol and Ben do this whenever they needed to show her some pictures. The phone and computer were now connected through the USB cable and Jessica turned on the phone. She selected and downloaded the picture of Carol. When the picture was loaded, she searched for the properties and wrote the data on a piece of paper. After erasing the photo from the hotel computer, she opened Google Earth and entered some of the data onto the map.

"Shit! I was right!" she murmured to herself.

She restarted the computer to ensure that any temporary data would be erased and went back upstairs to her room.

"My gut feeling was right. Call Pat and ask him if he could pick us up."

"What did you find?" asked Karen.

"You'll see... I need the proof first."

Karen called Pat who said he could be there in fifteen minutes.

"What's the 911 equivalent in this city?" asked Jessica.

Karen looked at the Hotel phone and noted the number for Police/Fire/Emergency.

"We may need to use this. Can you enter it into your cell as a Speed Dial number? I've done it already on mine."

"Wow! You sure know a lot about phones," marveled Karen.

"Being around Ben and Carol helped a lot. Let's go down to the lobby and wait for Pat."

"What about the suitcase? Do we leave it here?"

"Yes. No one will look under the bed. If they do come in here, they will riffle through my suitcase, which I put on the dresser," said Jessica.

Karen shook her head. "I've never walked away from a million dollars."

"This might be the only time," Jessica was not as worried.

They walked down to the lobby after hanging a 'Do Not Disturb' sign on the door. This was to protect against any hotel employees who may be overzealous in making up the room.

Pat drove up, accompanied by Len.

"Where should I take you?" he asked.

"Let's go to your apartment. I need to show you something," said Karen.

"What did they tell you?" asked Len.

"They asked for the money. I told them I didn't have it with me but could get it quickly."

"They didn't give you instructions for a drop off?" asked Pat.

"Not yet. I needed further proof and they gave it."

Traffic was not as heavy since rush hour was a few hours away.

"Can you stop at the next Police Station?" asked Karen.

"Police station?!" asked Pat incredulously. "Someone could be following us now. This is not safe. They warned you."

"I need to report some money stolen from my room. I didn't report it at the hotel since I don't trust them. Don't worry. I won't be long. I'll go in alone."

"I don't know, Jess. Pat knows a lot about this place. If the kidnappers told you not to go to the police you probably shouldn't."

"Its okay, Len. There is no danger," said Jessica.

Pat pulled into the parking lot of the police station. "Do you want me to come with you?"

"No, I'll be okay." Jessica jumped out and walked into the station.

"I hope she knows what she's doing. This could be very risky," said Pat.

"Don't worry, Jessica is smart. She doesn't take unnecessary risks," said Karen.

Karen herself was puzzled as to why Jessica went into the station. She knew that nothing had been stolen from her room. She trusted however, that what Jessica was doing was probably a good plan.

A few moments later she was back. "Sorry for the short notice. Should have told you before that some money was stolen from my room."

"That's a good hotel you're booked into. Things like that shouldn't happen there. You should have spoken to the Manager," said Pat.

"I will, when I get back."

There were a few cars parked in the lot as Pat pulled into his parking stall. "Did they tell you that they would meet you here?" asked Pat.

"No, but I will ask them to."

"But you don't have the money."

"They think I do."

Pat opened his apartment door and beckoned the women in. Len followed, panting after taking the few stairs up.

"Can I get you a drink?" asked Pat.

"No thanks, we've come to get Carol," Jessica responded.

"Did they tell you that they would bring her here?" asked Pat.

"No, but you can lead me to her, Pat."

Pat was startled. "How can I do that?"

"Because she is in this building," said Jessica.

"How do you know that? Why would they keep her here?"

"Karen, can you take out your phone and show the picture to Pat?"

"You see those drapes behind Carol?"

"Yes."

"They look a lot like yours, Pat," said Jessica.

Pat bristled. "She's not in this apartment, Jessica. Do you want to check it out?"

"Not in this apartment, but one of these apartments."

"That's ridiculous, Jessica! Those drapes are so common. Besides why would I hide Carol? I've got enough money. You are really making wild accusations. After all I've done for you!" snarled Pat.

"I checked the geotag on the photo that was just sent. The coordinates are for this area. The drapes confirm that it is this apartment building. They all have drapes like this. I can see it from the outside."

Pat's eyes narrowed. He looked at Len. "What kind of woman is this that you asked me to help, Len? She is accusing me of being a criminal."

Len stood up. He suddenly grabbed Jessica.

"Karen, the speed dial. Quick!"

Before Karen could hit the keys, Pat grabbed the phone and threw it across the room.

"Do you want your daughter back? If you do, sit down and listen to Len."

Len pushed her onto the sofa.

273

"Do you know what you did to me, Jessica?" he said as he panted and his face reddened.

"You destroyed my life. You sold out the company. It was my company too. I built it up with Ben and he promised me a share of it. Instead, you sold it to those incompetent people without even asking my advice! I have been living like a peasant for the last few years! I have taken low-paying jobs working for idiots because I could not find a job like I had in Guthrie Construction. I want my share! It should have been ten percent. Instead, all I asked for is one million, which I have to share with Pat and his friends. Kidnapping Carol was the only way I could get it from you. I don't mean to harm her. She was Ben's daughter."

"To commit a crime?! Is that what you have lowered yourself to?" shouted Jessica.

"Where is the money, Jessica?!" asked Pat. "All I need to do is make one phone call and she will be gone from here. You won't see her again if you don't cough up."

Jessica looked at Pat and then her gaze shifted to Len. He looked away and rubbed his sleeve on his sweaty face. She could sense he did not like this at all. However, it appeared that for Pat, this was routine business. *What a snake!*

"I want you to bring her to this apartment before I tell you. The money is not far from here."

Pat hesitated. Jessica looked steadily into his eyes. He was not used to confrontation with a woman. He had always been able to control them with his charm and good looks.

"I'm certain you and your men can make sure I can't escape from here without paying you. So, bring her here before I tell you."

"What do you think, Len?" asked Pat.

"Nobody should get hurt," said Len. "All of you stay here until Jessica and I get the money."

"I will take you there and give you the money. But we must have Carol first. I'll bet she is very close to us with your goons watching her."

Len looked at Pat. "Guess it should be okay. I don't want anyone getting hurt. I just want my money. My share of the company that she sold from under my nose."

"I don't know, Len. This woman seems too smart for her boots. She may pull a stunt."

"To think I trusted you! You low life!" sneered Karen.

"Maybe we can do it this way. We bring Carol here. Jessica and I go to where the money is hidden. She gives it to me. I phone you, Len, and then you can release Karen and Carol. They can take a cab to the hotel and you and I can get lost somewhere here in Thailand."

"Amateurs! I knew you would mess this up. Bring Carol now and you'd better run off," said Jessica.

"Why do you think we would do that?" said Pat.

They heard a thump outside. The door was kicked open and three police officers entered with guns drawn.

"Are these the men, Mrs. Guthrie?"

"Yes, if you can call them that. But first they need to take us to my daughter. She is in this apartment building. Tell me where, Pat. The game is up."

Pat and Len were stumped. Jessica was indeed too smart for them.

"How did you know she would be here?" asked Len.

"Pat assumed I knew nothing about GPS devices on phones. Your cellphone which you gave to your goons easily tracked to this address. The 'location' of the device was left on."

Pat looked at Len who nodded. They had been fooled by Jessica.

"Three floors up, Apartment 617. Knock three times and the door will be opened for you," said Pat. "Don't make too much commotion. I don't want anyone to get hurt."

"I'm coming with you, officer," said Jessica.

"Me too," Karen followed. "These losers will be in jail soon. Len, the jails in Thailand are not four-star."

Jessica, Karen and two officers went to the stairs. One remained with Pat and Len. Other apartment dwellers now opened their doors to see what the fuss was about, since they had heard the commotion. The police officer asked them to be quiet while they approached apartment 617. He walked to the door and gently knocked three times. It was opened and he quickly kicked it in and was followed by his colleague who pushed a man down to the floor.

Jessica and Karen rushed in and opened the door to the bedroom. Carol was there, tied to the iron bedposts with rope. Duct tape covered her mouth which Jessica quickly removed.

"Mum!"

Jessica hugged her wordlessly, tears streamed down her cheeks. Karen also joined with the hug.

"I'm okay, Mum."

"Oh Honey, I was so worried I wouldn't see you again." Jessica gently rubbed the rope marks on her wrists and stroked her cheeks. It was over. Finally. Carol was alive, her warm body pressed against hers. For a moment she recalled the fear when Jariya Panya had shown her Carol's photograph. She really thought she would not see her daughter again.

Carol stood up rubbed her wrists, shrugged her shoulders to remove her cramps from being restrained for so long and took a few steps towards the door. Jessica and Karen were on either side, holding her close, making sure that she wasn't snatched away again.

They passed the handcuffed man in the apartment and nodded thanks to the police officers.

"No worry, Mrs. Guthrie. Men go to jail now."

They walked down the stairs. Suddenly they heard a commotion in Pat's apartment. There was a shout and a sharp cry. Holding Carol's hand tightly, Jessica sprinted down the stairs and pushed open the door. Carol screamed at the sight.

Len lay on the floor with a kitchen knife in his abdomen. There was blood, lots of blood. His face was blue. The police officer was on the phone probably calling an ambulance. He spoke quickly in Thai and then told Jessica. "He grabbed knife and stabbed himself before I try stop him. I not expect him do that."

For a moment Jessica felt empathy for Len. He had gone downhill after Guthrie Engineering had been sold. He was a trusted friend of Ben's. Now he lay in a pool of blood which spread across the floor. It was not likely the ambulance would make it in time.

"Len! Can you hear me?"

"Yes," he wheezed. "I'm not fit to live anymore after what I did to Ben, to you and to Carol... I'm so sorry, Jessica. I thought it would be different. What I did was shameful. I just wanted my share. I didn't want anyone to get hurt."

Jessica did not know what to say. He had Carol kidnapped after all, but looking at this pale overweight man, lying on the floor, taking his last breaths was not easy. She held his hand, knowing that the end was near. "I'm sorry too. Ben would have been too. If only you had called me before I sold the company. I never realized how much pain it had caused you and the others."

She watched wordlessly as he coughed up blood. His eyes rolled back, his frame jerked and he was still. Jessica looked at Carol and then Karen. Pat looked away, unable to accept what had happened.

Chapter 51

It was the first night that Jessica slept soundly. Carol was with her now and that was all that mattered. The shock that Len had conspired to do this, still remained. He was Ben's right-hand man and it was inconceivable that he plotted to kidnap Carol. But the lack of money can make people do strange things. *What would I have done in a similar circumstance? Would I do harm to the child of my best friend if I was destitute?*

"Time to make a couple of visits, Honey."

"Where to, Mum?"

"We have to return your ransom money to the bank. I'll bet you'll never guess where it is?"

"Under the mattress?"

"Well, you are warm."

She pulled out the suitcase from under the bed and opened it to show Carol.

"Oh, my goodness. That is a lot of money. How much is in there, Mum?"

"Much less than what you are worth, Honey. It was horrible for me this last week. I had nightmares of who your kidnappers were, where they had you, if they had hurt you, or I dared not to think, if they had killed you already."

Mother and daughter held each other while tears rolled down their cheeks.

"Mum, they never hurt me. And they weren't rough with me either. I am pretty sure this was the first time they had done something like that. Maybe Len had told them not to hurt me. At no time, did I feel that they would kill me and they never ever threatened me. I was convinced they were amateurs."

"So was Pat. He put on a good act but made a big mistake. He forgot to instruct his cohorts in the most basic cellphone security. Anyway, let's not talk about him anymore. We have to get this money back to the bank. Or maybe I will ask them to pick it up from here."

She called Mr. Lee. "Hello, Mr. Lee. The suitcase you sent me doesn't belong to me. It must be another passenger's bag. Can you have your assistant come by and pick it up? I haven't removed anything."

"This must mean that Carol is back. Is that right, Mrs. Guthrie?"

"Yes, she is with me now. It has been quite an ordeal but she was not harmed."

"I am so happy and relieved, Mrs. Guthrie. There are a few bad apples in our community but most of us are very hospitable and kind as you may have found. I will send my man right away. Is there anything else I can do for you?"

"Yes, there is. I want to establish an education fund for a young boy. One of Carol's students. And I also want to set up a series of monthly payments for his living expenses, until he finishes school. Perhaps you can tell me how much this should be, so that he and his mother have a fairly comfortable life."

"Let me give it some thought, Mrs. Guthrie. We can meet again for your signature. That is very kind of you. He must be a very good student."

"Let's just say he is very special."

Jessica hung up the phone.

"Which student is this, Mum? There were about thirty in the class."

"I'm going to surprise you, and him. Let me call the Principal to set up a meeting tomorrow. I will make the call from Karen's room. Promise not to eavesdrop..."

The next day Anu was summoned to the principal's office. *Oh no, he will think I am fibbing if he hears that I was kidnapped again* he thought. *Or maybe he wants to punish me for missing school again.*

The secretary knocked on the door and opened it to let him in. He almost cried out in delight when he saw Miss Carol sitting there with her mother and her friend. Anu did not know what to say and stammered a 'Good Morning' but he could not hear what he said. His heart raced to see his idol safe with her mother.

Carol rose and hugged him. "Thank you, Anu. My mother and Mr. Suttikul told me how you helped and also about the way those men treated you. I am so glad that you are safe again with your mother."

Anu was still speechless. All he could do was to nod his head.

"Mr. Montri. There is one other thing. Mrs. Guthrie and Miss Carol will be paying your fees for the rest of the time you are in school here. Would you like to thank them?" Mr. Suttikul beamed at his student.

He nodded and once again blurted out a 'Thank you' of sorts.

"We have another surprise for you but you will hear about that in a few days. We are leaving for Canada this evening. Would you and your mother like to come to the airport with us to wish us goodbye?"

This time he had no problem speaking. "I am sad you leaving so soon but I will come to airport. My mother will be there also. I told her about you, Miss Carol."

"What did you tell her, Anu?"

Anu realized he had said too much already and it was more than obvious that he had been smitten. "I told her that I want to be teacher like you when I grow up."

Carol smiled and pinched his cheek. "I'm sure you did."

About the Author

John has written three books of short stories which are available in electronic and print edition on Amazon. Some of his short stories have been published in the Poetry Institute of Canada's annual anthologies.

John participated in Toastmaster International's Public Speaking Contests in the provinces of Alberta and Saskatchewan. In 1987, he won First Place at the Club, Area and Division levels in the Humorous Speech Contest, and in 1988 he won First Place for the same three levels for the International Speech Contest.

During an engineering career of four decades in the corporate world, John worked with some great characters. He has retired, and now lives in a small town in Alberta, Canada.

He plays the guitar and piano to entertain himself (but not others). For relaxation, he walks regularly under the blue skies of Alberta with his dogs, who give him the love and affection he needs. His wife and three children claim to love him too (sometimes).

Other books by J.G. Barrie

Beauty in the Beast and other musings

To the End of Love and other musings

The Lady in Red: An Anthology of Short Stories and other works

The Road from Mandalay-The Journeys of an Anglo-Indian Family

Made in the USA
Las Vegas, NV
31 July 2021